Ebby the Magnificent©

© 2022 Written and Illustrated by J. W. Julian
Map and sketches by John J.

Edited by Dianne M. Rich

Published by Ebby Books, LLC
www.JWJulian.com

The characters and events portrayed in this book are fictitious. Any similarity to real persons or creatures, living or dead, is coincidental and not intended by the author.

First Edition
Interior Design: The Killion Group, Inc. | www.TheKillionGroupInc.com
Digital ISBN 979-8-9866894-0-1
Print ISBN 979-8-9866894-1-8

Printed in Croatia by Denona d.o.o., www.denona.hr

THIS BOOK
BELONGS TO:
Jayven

Welcome to the Land of
Stones, little one. New
friends and adventures
are waiting inside.

Jessica W. Graham
7/5/23

DEDICATION

This Book is dedicated to my husband, John, whose kindness, love, friendship, and imagination were inspirations for this book, my mother, without whom I would not have been possible, Zoto, who encouraged me to pick up a paintbrush and paint with my heart, Team Ebby, consisting of Veselina and Mihaela, Amanda Z., and my dear sweet friends and family who have encouraged me in every aspect of this journey.

TABLE OF CONTENTS

The Land of Stones

The Tide Pools

Land of Dragons

The Big Sea

The Waterfall Caves

Drivenik Castle

Fluffle Valley

Skrufty's Forest

Slune

Napoleon's Farm

Stone Islands

River Slune

Roveen

Frisky's Rocks

Land of Stones

Bud Der's Farm

Zidani Island

John J ©
2021

Author's Note: This map is based on Ebby's descriptions of the Land of Stones as told to Frisky the Fox and shows the approximate locations of her adventures. JWJ

PART ONE

The Road to Roveen

CHAPTER ONE

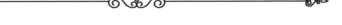

Ebby Meets Chip and Spot

*(In which Ebby makes friends and sees the world
beyond Fluffle Valley for the first time.)*

In a beautiful valley full of flowers and tall, sweet grass lived a
baby bunny named Ebby. Ebby lived in the Land of Stones
with her family in an underground bunny village called a
"fluffle". There were several fluffles in the valley, which is how
it became known as Fluffle Valley. Although lots of bunny
families lived in Ebby's fluffle, Ebby was not like the other
bunnies. She was an exceptional bunny who was going to do
amazing things.

Ebby was little compared to most other creatures in the valley, but she would not have it any other way. She loved being small. She could snuggle tightly under her mother's chin as she slept or dart through the tiniest holes when she played with her friends. Even though the grass grew high above her head, Ebby felt like a giant when she stood up on her back legs.

She could see much farther when she was standing, but always wondered if there was something else hiding just beyond her sight.

Ebby's favorite flowers were bright yellow. They playfully swayed from side to side as the wind swept through the valley floor and were yummy to eat. They gave her energy and made her happy. As much as Ebby loved eating the yummy yellow flowers, she never ate the red flowers with black centers that grew in Fluffle Valley. Her mother told her the red flowers would make her sleepy, and Ebby did not like to be sleepy. While all the other bunnies liked to take long naps, Ebby preferred to spend her time exploring the area around the fluffle.

The sky above the valley was deep blue during the day. Sometimes Ebby watched as white puffy clouds floated by high above her head. She imagined they were as soft and fluffy as her mother's fur. As the sun sank below the horizon at the end of each day, the sky became bright pink, red, orange, yellow, and purple. She loved watching the sun cross the sky. "One day," she said to herself, "I will follow the sun to see where it goes at night."

The sky became dark when the sun set, but it also came alive with tiny bright specks of shimmering light. Sometimes she could see her shadow at night from the light of the moon. The stars and moon reminded her there was light and life everywhere, even at night. She wondered where the moon and stars went during the day when she could not see them.

Each evening Ebby's friends came out of their burrows to eat dinner. Once they finished nibbling their fill of sweet grass and flowers they often played their favorite game called Hide and Peek. Hide and Peek was played by every baby bunny counting to ten at the same time then darting into a hole or under a bush to hide. Once hidden, the bunnies stayed still for as long as they could. If they felt brave, they would carefully stick their noses out of their hiding places and peek around to see if anyone was trying to find them. Since all the bunnies were hiding, no one was ever looking for anyone else. The game always ended with everyone going home alone after spending most of the evening hiding.

Ebby loved to be with her friends but thought a game about hiding was silly. She wanted to discover new things, not spend the evening hiding. Once she suggested instead of them all hiding, she could close her eyes while they hid and she would try to find them. "We can call it 'Hide and Seek'," she announced excitedly. But her friends did not want to be found. It sounded too scary; they preferred to keep playing Hide and Peek.

Ebby wished she could find someone who loved to explore and discover new things as much as she did, but none of her bunny friends were interested. They were too afraid to leave their parents' sight even for a moment. Their parents were also scared and constantly encouraged the babies to practice their hiding skills. Ebby did not understand why they were frightened. She was not afraid of anything.

One evening after dinner Ebby saw a furry figure off in the distance. Instead of a short, white, puffy tail like Ebby's, this creature had a long tail with a dark stripe running down his back. He stood on a log looking straight at Ebby. Even after her friends warned her to stay away from this unusual creature, she grabbed a yellow flower and dashed as quickly as she could to meet him. Ebby knew instantly they would become friends because she liked and respected everyone she met. As

Ebby got closer, she noticed the creature was not alone. He was talking to a little black bug covered with bright red dots. She overheard the bug say, "It's true! Ebby is the one I was telling you about." Ebby's ears perked up with curiosity. What one, she wondered?

The bug watched Ebby approach and straightened her wings to look presentable. "Hi, sweet thing," the little black bug said. "We've been waiting for you to visit us ever since we learned you were born. Everyone in Fluffle Valley is talking about you. We can't wait to find out where you will go and what you will do!"

Ebby did not know how to respond to this unusual greeting.

"I'm Spot, and this is my friend Chip." The bug pointed at the creature standing on the log with one of her wings. "He's a chipmunk. That's kind of like being a bunny, but not exactly the same."

Chip stopped chewing the nut he found earlier and put it in his upper cheek for later. "Ebby, it's so wonderful to finally meet you! We've heard so much about you, but true to your name you've been pretty elusive." Ebby did not know how they knew who she was or what elusive meant.

Ebby dropped the yellow flower she held in her mouth at Chip's feet so she could respond to them. "It's super nice to meet you both. I brought you this yummy yellow flower and I hope you like it as much as I do. How do you know who I am, and what does elusive mean?"

Chip and Spot giggled a little bit because they thought it was funny Ebby did not know she was an Elusive Baby Bunny. "Elusive," said Chip, "means you are really hard to find. And because you are elusive everyone wants to find you.

Unbelievable things happen when an Elusive Baby Bunny like you is born."

 This confused Ebby. She had never been called an Elusive Baby Bunny before and had no idea what they were talking about. "I'm hard to find?" She wrinkled up her nose and tilted her head. "But I'm always exactly where I am."

This made Chip laugh so hard he almost fell off the log. "Just because *you* know where you are, doesn't mean anyone else does! Elusive Baby Bunnies never stay in the same place for long because they want to experience everything. As soon as an Elusive Baby Bunny finishes exploring one place, they want to start a new adventure in another place right away. This makes it difficult to find them."

Ebby still did not understand why they called her an Elusive Baby Bunny, but at that moment she was more curious about why Chip was standing on the log. "What are you doing on that log?" Ebby asked.

"I have a better view of the valley from up here than I do from the ground," Chip replied. "There is an entire world just beyond the edge of where you can see. That's why you can see farther away when you're standing on your hind legs than on all fours. I can see even farther when I'm standing on this log."

Ebby always suspected there was something more to see just out of her sight. She loved standing up on her back legs because she could almost see over the top of the grass, but she had never stood on a log before. "Can I come up there on your log with you?"

"Of course!" said Chip. "But be aware if you're anything like the Elusive Baby Bunnies who came before you, this will be the first of many steps you take to see the world."

Chip moved over to give her room as Ebby jumped up on the log. She wobbled around a bit until she found a spot wide enough to stand up. Slowly she stood on her hind legs. Her eyes widened at what she saw. She had been right all along. There really was an entire world just above the tall grass and beyond the edge of where she could see.

Standing on the log she saw over the tops of her favorite yellow flowers and tall grass for the first time in her life. The ~~...~~ There were trees larger than the biggest flowers she had ever seen. Tall mountains loomed high over Fluffle Valley far off in the distance. She could not believe she had not seen them before. The sun was going down behind the mountains and she immediately realized that was where the sun went at night. Closer to her, she saw strange white structures with red tops dotting the hills. She saw creatures in the fields far off in the distance who looked much different than anyone she knew.

"That's marvelous!" Ebby exclaimed. "I want to see everything there is to see and go everywhere there is to go!" This was exactly what Chip and Spot expected an Elusive Baby Bunny to say.

CHAPTER TWO

Ebby, the Elusive Baby Bunny

*(In which Ebby learns what it means to
be an Elusive Baby Bunny.)*

E bby turned around in time to see Chip and Spot smiling at each other. Her eyes were wide with wonder, and she felt her heart beating faster and faster. She wiggled her fluffy white tail as she always did when she was excited. More than anything she wanted to jump off the log and scurry towards the mountains to see where the sun was going next. She took several deep breaths to calm down before she was ready to speak. "What is that place over there? What are those white and red boxes? What are those large creatures?" She had so many questions she could hardly contain herself.

Chip tried his best to answer her. "The white boxes with red tops are houses like the one you live in, but instead of being underground like your home, they're built above ground. And instead of bunnies, creatures called humans live in them. Humans stand on two legs and don't have tails, long ears, or fur. The large creatures standing in the fields are cows and horses. They're furry like us but are much larger. For the most part cows and horses just eat grass."

Ebby also ate grass, but not nearly as much as cows and horses.

"Have you been to the other side of the valley?" Ebby asked Chip and Spot.

"No, I haven't." Chip responded. "It's too far for me to go. It would take several days to get there, and I'm not sure I could find my way home."

"I haven't been there either," Spot chimed in. Just as she said that, a small gust of wind blew her off the log. "The winds are too hard for me to fly through. I might never make it back." She landed gracefully on the log next to Chip.

Ebby could not understand Chip and Spot's reasons for not going. Too far? Too challenging? Those were the reasons she wanted to go there the instant she saw across the valley. She could not wait to travel to the other side of the valley, no matter how long it took her to get there.

The sun was now hidden completely behind the mountains and it was starting to get dark. Ebby knew she needed to get back home before her mother started worrying about her. She thanked Chip and Spot and jumped off the log. Her fluffy white tail became a blur as she moved quickly through the grass and flowers on her way back home.

As soon as she saw her mother, Ebby gushed out what Chip and Spot taught her, including them calling her an Elusive Baby Bunny. "Have you ever stood on a log? Have you seen the mountains? Do you know that's where the sun goes at night? Do you know about humans and their houses? They don't live underground like we do." She could barely contain herself and ran circles around her mother as she blurted out questions. "Did you know there are cows and horses that are like big bunnies?"

19

Her mother smiled tenderly down at her. "Calm down a bit, Ebby, so I can talk to you." Ebby stopped running and waited impatiently for her mother to speak.

Ebby's mother had heard about the outside world but had never seen it herself. Now that Ebby had discovered it, she knew it was time to tell Ebby the truth about being an Elusive Baby Bunny. She took a deep breath, "I've never been to the outside world, but my parents taught me about Elusive Baby Bunnies when I was little. Like everyone else in Fluffle Valley, I grew up hearing stories about their amazing adventures. I never imagined they were real, let alone that one of my own children would be one. I thought they were just stories our parents taught us so we would be nice to everyone we met. But then you were born, and I understood for the first time that Elusive Baby Bunnies are real.

"Chip and Spot are right. You are an Elusive Baby Bunny. The EBB in your name is short for Elusive Baby Bunny. You're one of the rarest bunnies ever born in the world. Most baby bunnies are timid and scared. That's why they always want to play Hide and Peek. They stay close to their parents and most never leave their fluffle, even when they grow up. But sometimes a baby bunny is born with a fearless and kind heart. This special baby is known as an Elusive Baby Bunny. There is only one Elusive Baby Bunny alive in the entire world at any one time. This doesn't happen often, and no one knows exactly when and where that bunny will appear. Sometimes hundreds of years pass without an Elusive Baby Bunny being born.

"My parents told me that Elusive Baby Bunnies love to travel the world. They never stay in any one place for long before they want to go somewhere else. This makes it hard to find them and that's why they are called elusive." Ebby noticed this was the same thing Chip said about Elusive Baby Bunnies. "They make friends everywhere they go because they have the purest of hearts. And they are incapable of being mean or cruel because they cannot stand to see anyone sad."

Ebby's mother snuggled closer to her. "I knew you were an Elusive Baby Bunny the moment you were born. Your eyes were wide open, and you were covered with a thick coat of soft brown fur. You began running around the burrow a few minutes after you were born. Ordinary baby bunnies don't open their eyes or move around until several weeks after they are born. You were fearless and liked to explore and ask questions from the beginning. I didn't tell you that you're an Elusive Baby Bunny or anything about the outside world because I knew when you learned the truth you would want to leave Fluffle Valley and discover the world. I've never left the fluffle, and I wanted to keep you home as long as possible."

21

Ebby did not fully understand what being an Elusive Baby Bunny entailed, but it finally made sense to her why she was not like other bunnies.

"You'll have to wait until the morning to hear more. It's late and we need to go to bed." Ebby snuggled close to her mother and fell asleep knowing there was an entire world beyond the flowers. That night, Ebby knew Fluffle Valley looked like this:

And not like this:

The next morning, before the sun rose, Ebby woke her mother to ask her what else she knew about Elusive Baby Bunnies and the outside world. Her mother was tired and not ready to get up. "Go ask Chip and Spot. Almost everyone knows stories about Elusive Baby Bunnies." She closed her eyes again. "They should be able to tell you some." Ebby rubbed noses with her mother before leaving.

Chip was standing on his log eating a nut and Spot was nibbling on a piece of grass when Ebby arrived. "Can you tell me more about the outside world?"

Chip quickly swallowed the rest of his nut and replied, "I don't know much because I've never been there myself, but I'll tell you what I know. Take a seat." When Ebby was sitting comfortably he told her what he knew about the world outside their valley. "I've overheard bits and pieces of information from travelers resting nearby. I usually go over to see if they have something tasty to eat. I've heard them describe places where water flows from inside the mountains and where humans live on pieces of land surrounded by water. None of it made any sense to me because we don't have that in Fluffle Valley."

It did not make any sense to Ebby either. How did water get inside of a mountain? How did land end up in the middle of water? She wanted to see it for herself.

"What can you tell me about Elusive Baby Bunnies? My mother said you might know some stories."

Chip and Spot never thought they would have the honor of telling Elusive Baby Bunny stories to a real live Elusive Baby Bunny. This was something they would remember for the rest of their lives.

CHAPTER THREE

Rebby the Gallant

*(In which Ebby hears an amazing story
about another Elusive Baby Bunny.)*

Chip cleared his throat before beginning their favorite story about Rebby the Gallant. "Rebby was born long ago in a land far from Fluffle Valley. No one knows exactly where he was from because everyone wanted to claim him as one of their own. Some said he came from a place called The Land of Dragons. Others said he came from The Land of Roses. No one knows for sure where he came from but it's certain he traveled to both places.

"He wasn't born with the name Rebby the Gallant. His parents simply called him Rebby because they didn't know what sort of Elusive Baby Bunny he would become. For thousands of years Elusive Baby Bunnies have been named by the ones who were personally touched by their kindness. Rebby became known as "Rebby the Gallant" because of his fearless exploits. He didn't consider himself to be particularly brave, but that's the way of Elusive Baby Bunnies. One of their most beloved characteristics is that they are humble."

Spot, eager for Chip to get to her favorite part of the story,

bumped him with her wing. Chip got the hint and skipped the rest of his background speech about Elusive Baby Bunny traits. "Early one spring Rebby traveled through a deep and narrow valley in the mountains. The valley was surrounded by steep rock cliffs on either side. Every spring the sun warmed the valley and melted the snow high up in the mountains. The melting snow collected at the bottom of the mountains forming a large river that flowed through the middle of the valley floor. A small village sat along the banks where humans, cows, and horses lived.

"For hundreds of years the river flowed past the village without difficulty. Eventually the villagers built a stone bridge over the river so they could build houses and farms on both sides of the river. That winter, there had been a lot of snow in the mountains. As the snow melted, the river became deep and flowed faster than before.

Rebby followed the river on his way to the village until a thunderstorm turned the skies black and rain poured down as he had never seen before. Bolts of lightning crackled through the sky, and the roar of thunder bounced from cliff to cliff. Rebby sprinted for the village hoping to find shelter until the storm passed. He reached the village when, without warning, the biggest bolt of lightning ever seen in all the world, struck the cliff above the village with a mighty blow that sent a huge boulder hurtling down the valley floor directly towards Rebby and the village." Chip abruptly stopped talking.

Ebby looked up at Chip with her mouth open and her ears pointing straight at him. She had seen thunder and lightning in Fluffle Valley, but nothing like the storm Chip described. "What happened to Rebby?" Ebby squeaked. Her tail started to wiggle in nervous anticipation.

Chip smiled. This was his favorite part of the story. He paused to let the suspense build. The longer he waited, the faster Ebby's tail went until her entire back side was moving from side to side. Spot noticed the worry on Ebby's face and hit Chip with her wing again. "Do you want me to finish the story, Chip?" she said sternly like a mother scolding her child.

Chip winked at Spot as he pretended to forget what he was saying. "Now how did the rest of the story go?" He knew he was never going to get to tell an Elusive Baby Bunny a story like this again in his life and wanted to make it last.

"Chip, what happened to Rebby?!" Ebby repeated. Her voice was even higher this time.

Chip started where he left off. "The boulder shook the earth as it thundered down the mountain. It crushed large trees and everything else in its path. Rebby jumped out of its way as it passed. The boulder came to a rest in the middle of the river, a short distance below the stone bridge. It was followed by an avalanche of smaller rocks that dammed up the river. Rebby watched as the river started to back up behind the boulder threatening to flood the village and destroy the bridge. The villagers ran to see what had caused the tremendous noise. The boulder was larger than their homes, and the water was rising quickly. They didn't have any way to move the boulder and save the village."

Tears started to form in Ebby's eyes as she listened in silence to the threat to the villagers and their homes. If they could not move the boulder then the village would be destroyed. Even though Ebby wanted to learn more about Elusive Baby Bunnies, she did not want to hear this sad story. "That's enough, Chip. I can't bear to hear any more."

Chip and Spot saw the tears in her eyes. If there had been any question whether Ebby was an Elusive Baby Bunny, her tears removed all doubt from their minds. Elusive Baby Bunnies were well-known for their inability to see someone else suffer or be sad. "Wait," said Spot, "we haven't gotten to the part where you learn how Rebby became known as Rebby the Gallant. Trust us, and let us finish his story." Ebby sniffed and wiped her tears with her front paws. She nodded for Chip to proceed with the story.

"Rebby knew the villagers wouldn't be able to move the boulder in time by themselves. It was simply too large, and the water was building up too quickly. Without a thought to his own safety, Rebby darted around the rock to the lower side of the boulder and started digging furiously with his front paws. The villagers watched in stunned silence as the little baby bunny started flicking tiny amounts of sand, gravel, and stones from the river bed directly underneath the boulder.

"Rebby knew he couldn't move the boulder by himself. But Rebby, like all bunnies, excelled at digging. He thought if he could dig a tunnel under the boulder, the water would start flowing through it. If enough water flowed under the boulder, the force of the water could dislodge the rock and break up the dam. Anyway, he thought it was worth a try. He couldn't just sit on his haunches and watch the villagers lose their homes.

"Inch by inch Rebby advanced under the boulder. He was muddy and exhausted, but he couldn't stop. The villagers were depending on him. He dug a narrow tunnel under the boulder large enough for him to move through, but that's all the space he needed. He didn't know what was happening outside or how long he'd been digging when he felt the ground under him getting wetter and turning to mud.

"Then he felt a trickle of water running between his feet. He got a burst of energy knowing he was getting close to the front of the boulder. He dug even faster, and the trickle became a stream. Covered in mud he had a hard time seeing anything in the narrow tunnel, but still he didn't stop. Suddenly he was hit in his face with a blast of cold water from the river. He had made it to the upper side of the boulder. The water pushed him all the way through his narrow tunnel, taking the loose dirt along with him. He closed his eyes tightly and held his breath as he catapulted out of the tunnel. The force of the water hurled Rebby onto a big patch of grass on the side of the river. He jumped up the second he landed and scurried up the river bank to safety.

"Rebby and the villagers watched in awe as the water shot through his tiny tunnel. More and more water found its way through the tunnel until the water was roaring underneath the boulder, taking all the smaller rocks with it. Finally, the boulder began to move. It started sluggishly at first as the water upstream began pushing on the boulder from underneath. Then the boulder was pushed from one side to the other until it started rolling downstream. The river continued to push the rock until the water, which had been threatening to overflow the river banks and flood the village, flowed harmlessly past the village once again. Rebby had saved the village."

As Chip finished telling the story, Spot dabbed her eyes with her wings to stop the tears. It did not matter how many times she heard this story, it always choked her up. Ebby felt a huge wave of relief pour over her. "Is it possible? Did Rebby save the village?"

Spot cleared her throat before answering Ebby. She did not want Ebby to think she was a silly old bug who cried at happy endings. "Of course it's true! That's what makes Elusive Baby Bunnies so special. No one ever expects something so extraordinary from a baby bunny. Even today if you go to that valley you will see the giant boulder in the middle of the river, downstream from the village. They call it 'Rebby's Rock.'"

At first, Ebby could not believe a little baby bunny like herself saved an entire village. The more she thought about it, the more she realized that she would have done the same thing. She just hoped she would be nearby when something terrible like that happened so she could help as Rebby did.

CHAPTER FOUR

Ebby Meets Napoleon Ponyparte

*(In which Ebby discovers kindness
is a gift on its own.)*

Ebby always woke up early to watch the sun rise over Fluffle Valley. It was magical to see the sky become bright pink and the rays of the sun turn the land a golden glow. She usually ate a breakfast of grass and flowers then helped her mother with the chores back at the burrow. After chores she would explore the fluffle all day while her friends stayed safely inside their burrows until it was time for dinner. After seeing the outside world, learning about Rebby the Gallant's heroic acts, and learning she was an Elusive Baby Bunny, Ebby no longer wanted to explore the area around the fluffle. She wanted to see everything there was to see and do everything there was to do. She could not help it because she was an Elusive Baby Bunny.

Two days after standing on Chip's log, Ebby told her mother she wanted to explore the world and see where the sun went at night. Her mother knew this would eventually happen because Ebby was an Elusive Baby Bunny. Although she would miss Ebby terribly and wished she would stay at home forever, she did not try to stop her from leaving. She knew Ebby would make the world a better place, just as the Elusive Baby Bunnies before her had done. "Ebby, you are an exceptionally rare bunny," her mother said lovingly. "Always remember to be kind and helpful to everyone you meet."

"I will, Mother, I promise." Ebby gave her mother one last nose rub before leaving to say goodbye to the rest of her fluffle.

Afterwards she headed to where she saw the sun set between the mountains. She did not know exactly where she was going, but she knew the world must be full of delightful creatures and they were waiting beyond the horizon to become her friends.

At first the ground was covered with the same tall, sweet grass and yellow flowers that grew near her fluffle. After some time, more red sleepy flowers appeared than where she grew up as well as lots of other flowers, which did not grow near her fluffle. She avoided eating the red sleepy flowers but enjoyed trying the new small white and pink flowers she discovered along the path. The grass growing in this part of the valley also tasted slightly different. It was all new and wonderful.

By the time the sun started going down she was exhausted. She spent the first night tucked in a tight little ball under a bush. Even though she was far away from home she found comfort in the familiar night sky. The moon and stars were like a piece of home she could take on her adventures.

Early the next morning she woke abruptly to a strange sound close to her head. She thought she had fallen asleep far away from anything or anyone, but looking around with drowsy eyes she saw she was in a fenced field. A big brown four-legged creature was eating grass a few feet away from where she had been sleeping. "Good morning," she said jumping to her feet. "I am Ebby. What is your name?"

"I am Napoleon Ponyparte," he said startled by the brave baby bunny's confidence.

"Hello, Napoleon, I've never seen anyone quite like you before. Are you a cow or a horse?"

"I'm a horse." He threw his nose in the air and neighed softly in amusement because no one had ever asked him that before. "It's nice to meet you, Ebby." He lowered his head to the ground so she could rub his nose. His nose was soft, warm, and velvety, and his breath smelled like sweet grass. He was tall and strong with beautiful dark brown eyes. The back of his neck was covered with long flowing black hair that became blue and purple in the sunshine. His tail was also black and stretched almost to the ground. Napoleon was the most impressive creature she had ever seen.

"What are you doing out here all by yourself?" Napoleon asked with a bit of concern in his voice.

"I'm on a journey to see the world. I want to see where the sun goes at night, where the stars and moon go during the day, and everything else I can possibly see. I've only just begun and it's already incredible." Remembering what her mother told her about being kind and helpful to everyone she met, she asked, "Is there anything I can do to make your day better?"

Napoleon shook his head lightly, tossing his long, beautiful mane from side to side, and snorted softly. No one had been this kind to him for a long time. "Would you like to spend a little time with me before you continue your journey?"

"I would love to." Ebby said sitting up on her hind legs. Not seeing any other horses in the field, she asked Napoleon, "Do you live here alone?"

"There are some other horses on the farm, but they are all out working in the fields now. I'm alone during the day."

Ebby thought about all the other bunnies living in her fluffle. Even though they did not like to explore with her, they were always close. "That must be lonely."

"It can be sometimes, but I'm an older horse so I'm not as helpful around the farm as I was when I was younger. You should have seen me in my youth." Napoleon's gaze drifted into the distance. "I used to play all day in the fields with my friends, seeing who could run the fastest or jump the highest. When I got older a boy named Kristof took me from the fields and brought me to this farm. I used to help him clear and plow the fields. After the harvest I pulled his cart to the village over the mountains. Sometimes after we finished our work for the day, he rode on my back for fun. I loved it when I ran so fast I could hear the wind blowing through my ears. It was hard work but I loved doing things with Kristof."

Napoleon's voice took on a somber tone. "He doesn't ride me anymore or have me pull his cart to the village. Now the younger horses get to spend time with him like I used to do." Ebby imagined Napoleon running through the fields with his mane flowing through the wind.

"One of the things I miss the most is the time we used to spend together after a long day of work. Kristof brushed me down and put a warm blanket over my back at the end of each day. Sometimes he gave me carrots as a special treat and rubbed my nose as I ate them."

"What is a carrot?" Ebby asked.

"Jump on my back and I'll show you." Napoleon lowered himself down as far as he could. With a little help from Napoleon, Ebby managed to get up on Napoleon's back. The view from Napoleon's back was much better than standing on Chip's log. She saw farther than she thought possible. The ground was so far away from where she sat. She tried to spot her fluffle, but all she saw was a field of flowers and grass stretching as far as she could see. Resolved to continue her adventure, she turned back around to see where Napoleon was taking her.

Napoleon walked carefully. He did not want to drop his precious rider. He walked across the field to a big stone barn. "This is where Kristof used to brush me down at night after a long day of work." He leaned next to an open window. "Go ahead and jump onto the ledge." After she landed safely, Ebby watched Napoleon walk into the building. It was dark inside and smelled like dirt and old dried grass. He came back a few moments later with several long orange objects with bright green leaves dangling from his mouth. He set them on the ledge next to Ebby.

"These are carrots. They were my favorite thing to eat when I was young, but I can't eat them anymore. They're too hard on my teeth, but I think you will enjoy them."

Ebby sniffed them first then started nibbling on the long green leaves. They tasted all right but not as good as a yummy yellow flower. Ebby ate all the leaves, not wanting to disappoint Napoleon. She stopped eating at the unfamiliar orange part.

Napoleon snickered, his beautiful brown eyes smiling. "Now try the orange part. *That's* the good stuff." Ebby cautiously nibbled on the orange part of the carrot. It was crunchy and hard. She nibbled a little more. She liked the way it tasted and how it felt in her mouth. It was strange. New. Exotic. She took a couple of bigger bites. It was sweet, flavorful, and crunchy. It was delicious.

Ebby had never heard of a carrot before. They did not grow near her fluffle so she doubted her mother had eaten one either. She would definitely bring her mother some carrots when she went back home.

Napoleon watched Ebby nibble on the carrot. He was delighted to see how much she enjoyed it. Ebby stopped chewing again. It broke her heart to know he could not eat his favorite food. She thought about how she would feel if she could not eat yummy yellow flowers anymore. Without hesitation she started taking bigger bites from the remaining carrots and put them next to her on the ledge until all the carrots were in a pile of small bunny-bite-sized pieces. Napoleon watched Ebby with curiosity. He concluded it must be an odd bunny custom.

When she finished, she turned to Napoleon and told him, "These are for you. I bit them into smaller pieces so they will be easier for you to eat. Thank you so much for teaching me about carrots, telling me about your life, and for being so kind to me. My mother was right. The most important thing you can do is be kind and helpful to everyone you meet."

Napoleon stood silently for a few moments without moving. No one had ever done this for him before. Although Kristof still gave him carrots from time to time, he had not noticed Napoleon did not eat them and instead left them for the younger horses. Napoleon was touched that Ebby not only remembered he could not eat carrots anymore, but bit them into smaller pieces so *he* could eat them.

He picked up a few of the bunny-bite-sized pieces with his lips and chewed on them a few times before swallowing. The flavor of the carrots brought back memories of his earlier days. He remembered kicking up his hooves with his friends, jumping over creeks and bushes, and running so fast the wind sang in his ears. He nibbled a few more pieces. "You are no ordinary creature, Ebby. You are *magnificent*! Thank you so much for reminding me what it was like to be young and how easy it is to be kind. Stopping on your journey to spend some time with me was the most precious gift of all."

Ebby rubbed her little nose against Napoleon's and said, "I don't know any other way to be."

Napoleon took his time eating the rest of the carrot pieces, savoring the flavor in each bite. He continued to tell Ebby stories of his youth until he grew tired. "This is what happens when you get older, Ebby," he said apologetically. "You slow down and want to rest at the oddest times. That's why you should do what you can when you're young and have energy. You will have plenty of time to slow down when you get older."

Ebby had not mentioned that she was an Elusive Baby Bunny when she introduced herself to Napoleon. If she had, Napoleon would have known she had been an unstoppable bundle of energy from the moment she was born. Ebby did not know if she was ever going to slow down, but she was ready to see the world and knew Napoleon needed to rest. "Thank you for sharing your stories with me, Napoleon. I've got a long way to go on my journey and I better get started now if I am going to learn where the sun goes at night."

Napoleon nodded in agreement. "The first village you'll come to on the other side of the mountain is called Slune. I used to take a cart full of supplies to the villagers there." He leaned close to the window ledge again and lowered his head for her to jump on to his back. "Slune is old and unlike any other village I have seen. It's the perfect place to continue your journey."

Napoleon walked to the fence at the far end of the field. He knelt down to let Ebby jump to the ground. Dropping two carrots at her feet, he pointed at a small trail to the right with his nose. "Follow that trail to Slune. You should be able to get there by tomorrow morning."

"I will never forget you, Napoleon!" Ebby stated as she started down the trail to her next adventure.

Napoleon whinnied and shook his head softly. "And I will never forget you, *magnificent Ebby*!"

CHAPTER FIVE

Ebby, Nikola, and the Wondrous Village of Slune

(In which Ebby helps a young boy make friends.)

Ebby hopped cheerfully as the trail twisted its way through the valley. She stopped often to study the new birds, trees, and flowers along the way. Gradually the trail sloped upwards as it led her into the mountains. Fluffle Valley got smaller and smaller in the distance until it disappeared completely from her sight.

When Ebby finally reached the top of the mountain she climbed onto a big rock to see what was ahead. The view was breathtaking. She saw villages, rivers, and forests far below her. In the distance a castle seemed to hover in the sky.

She followed the path down the mountain towards Slune. A river flowed downhill alongside the path in a series of waterfalls and small pools. As the evening approached she found a puddle of cool water where a family of bright blue butterflies played happily in the fading sunlight. Several birds and lizards gathered around the area as well. An unusually shaped stone lay in the center of the water. It looked old and forgotten.

Ebby joined the others at the edge of the pond and drank the cold clear water. It was refreshing after her long journey over the mountain. She ate one of the carrots Napoleon gave her. Together the sound of the water flowing, the birds singing, and the butterflies tittering made her sleepy. She found a soft bed of moss and curled up. Her eyelids grew heavy as she watched the last rays of the sun fade into the night. This was the best day of her little life. She fell into a deep sleep, dreaming about sweet Napoleon running through the fields, his mane flowing in the wind.

She arose early the next morning and hopped the short distance to Slune. The houses in the village were made of brick and stone and were built on top of several rivers and waterfalls, which flowed down from the mountains. As she neared the village, Ebby saw water running through and under many of the buildings. Some had large wooden wheels attached to them. The wheels turned as the water flowed over them. Ebby did not know what these wooden wheels were but made a mental note to ask. She had never been to a village of any sort before, let alone one as striking as Slune. This must be what Napoleon meant when he said it was unlike any other village he had seen.

Two-legged fur-less creatures, who Ebby assumed were humans, walked on stone paths between the buildings. Others walked over bridges made of stones and wood. Some carried heavy bags on their backs or walked alongside horses pulling carts loaded with similar bags. Smaller humans ran through the cobblestone streets and played together in the water.

As she got closer, Ebby saw a small human sitting alone on a wooden dock with his feet dangling below him. He stared at the water holding a stick with a string tied to it. The other end of the string floated in the water below. He was crying softly. She hopped up to the little human and stood up on her hind legs. "Hi. I'm Ebby. What's your name? Here is a carrot my friend Napoleon Ponyparte gave me. I want you to have it. Eat the orange part, it's scrumptious. What are you doing? Why are you crying?" The questions spilled out of her so rapidly in her excitement he did not have a chance to respond. She stood breathlessly waiting for him to answer.

The little human turned in surprise to look at Ebby and wiped the tears from his face. A bunny had never spoken to him before, let alone given him a carrot. "Hi Ebby, I'm Nikola. I'm fishing." He stared at the end of his pole hoping to see it move, but it remained perfectly still. "I'm trying to catch the big purple sea dragon that's supposed to live in the water. No one's seen it for many years but maybe I'll get lucky and catch it."

"Are you sad because you haven't caught the dragon yet?"

"No, I'm sad because we just moved to Slune and I don't have any friends here. Nothing is the same. The food, language, clothes, and everything else is different. The other kids make fun of me because of the way I dress and talk. If I catch the purple sea dragon maybe they'll want to be my friend."

This did not make any sense to Ebby. She thought about her friendships with Chip, Spot, and Napoleon. They all ate different food, had different tails, looked and sounded different. This made them more interesting to her, not less interesting. She might never have found out about the world outside of Fluffle Valley without Spot and Chip's help. She might never have tasted carrots or found Slune without Napoleon's help. Each new friend she made taught her something meaningful. She could not understand why the other little humans did not want to play with Nikola.

"Maybe the problem is they don't know you." She thought

of her own fluffle. She and her friends did not play with bunnies from other fluffles. She never thought about it before. There were probably some bunnies back home who were just as lonely as Nikola, and she never knew it. "I'll play with you, Nikola. We'll have so much fun!"

Nikola smiled at Ebby. He now had a soft, furry, sweet friend who gave him carrots and wanted to spend time with him. He put his fishing pole down in a safe place and they left the dock to explore the village together. The first thing Ebby did was teach Nikola how to play Hide and Seek. By taking turns hiding and finding each other they were able explore all sorts of places in the village Nikola had never seen before. Afterwards, they ran across the bridges, hopped over the rocks, and told each other stories about their lives. They did not care that they came from different backgrounds, sounded different, looked different, and ate different food. They played all day long.

When it started getting dark, Nikola invited Ebby to his home for dinner and to meet his parents. They made their way through the village until they came to Nikola's house at the edge of town. It was made entirely of stone and a small river flowed beside it. A large wooden wheel was attached to the house like the ones she had seen earlier in the day. The water from the river flowed over the spokes of the wheel, which caused the wheel to turn. The creaking of the wooden wheel could be heard over the sound of rushing water.

They walked over a small bridge to a big wooden door. Nikola opened the door and held it open for Ebby to pass. The house was warm, bright, and full of wonderful new smells. It was nothing like Ebby's burrow. He introduced Ebby to his parents, Victoria and Alex. They were overjoyed Nikola had made a friend and invited Ebby to stay the night. Ebby had never slept in a house before and was eager to have another new experience.

They sat down at a big wooden table to eat dinner. Ebby was too small to sit in a chair to eat, so she sat on the table next to Nikola. Victoria smiled uncertainly as she placed a plate full of carrots in front of Ebby. "I hope you like carrots. I wasn't expecting Nikola to bring a friend home for dinner and didn't have time to make anything special for you."

"Thank you, I love carrots," she said wiggling her tail with glee. Ebby thought about her mother and Napoleon as she nibbled on them. "Can you tell me what the large, wooden wheel on the side of your house is for?"

Nikola's father responded and pointed towards the back

of the house where the wheel was located. "We use it to make flour. The force of the river's current rotates the wheel. When the wheel is moving, it turns large stones, which grind wheat into flour. That's why our village is built on rivers and waterfalls. Almost every house can grind its own flour." Alex took a bite of his dinner.

"What is wheat and flour?" Ebby asked because they did not have them in her fluffle.

"Wheat is a type of grass," he said, "but different than the grass you eat. We take the seeds and grind them into a fine powder called flour. You probably saw people carrying large bags in the streets. They were carrying either wheat or flour to sell in the market square."

"What do you do with the flour?" Ebby asked.

"The flour is used to make bread and other tasty treats the villagers like to eat." Victoria held up a piece of the bread she made earlier that day, "Would you like to try a piece?" Ebby nodded eagerly and wiggled her tail again. Victoria gave her a warm piece of bread dripping with melted butter and a sweet mixture of berries on top. It was more delicious than the carrots.

When it was time to go to sleep, Victoria gave Ebby a soft pillow and set it on the floor next to Nikola's bed. Nikola fell asleep with a smile on his face and his hand hanging below his bed so he could pet Ebby's soft fur. He slept better than he had since they moved to Slune.

The next morning Nikola and Ebby went outside to play after breakfast. Four boys from the village waited for them in front of Nikola's house, led by the oldest boy, Deni. They had heard about the unusual boy with a strange accent, funny clothes, and his "pet baby bunny." They wanted to see the boy and his bunny for themselves.

Ebby stood up on her hind legs and greeted the boys warmly. "Hi, I'm Ebby and this is Nikola. He's my friend, and if you give him a chance, he will become your friend too." Deni and his friends were stunned by this brave and confident little baby bunny. It was obvious that Ebby was not a simple pet bunny. If Ebby and Nikola could be friends when they were so different, the four boys realized they could be Nikola's friends too.

Instead of making fun of Nikola and teasing him about his "pet baby bunny" like they had set out to do, the boys from Slune gave Nikola and Ebby a chance to get to know them. First, Ebby and Nikola taught them how to play Hide and Seek. They loved playing it because they explored places around Slune none of them had ever gone before trying to find the best hiding place. Each game was like a miniature adventure. Ebby enjoyed the anticipation of finding someone who was trying to stay hidden as much as she enjoyed the thrill of being found. Most importantly, she cherished having friends who liked to explore as much as she did.

After playing Hide and Seek for some time, the boys took Nikola and Ebby to their favorite place to play by a large waterfall. Soon they were all wet and exhausted. As they sat down in the sun to catch their breath, Nikola told them about the village where he grew up and the delicious treats his mother cooked. He also taught them some words that were not used in Slune. The boys from Slune had fun trying to pronounce the new words and teased each other for not saying them correctly.

Later they sat on the dock wishing the mysterious purple sea dragon would return. Nikola pulled out his fishing pole and threw the string back in the water. Deni explained the history of the dragon to Ebby. "Many years ago a great purple sea dragon swam up the river to Slune from the Big Sea. Everyone was so frightened they ran away and hid. They never came out from hiding and eventually the dragon left. The villagers later learned it was a magical dragon named Sofia. They still regret running away from her and hope that she will come back some day and give them another chance. It is said that good things will happen if she returns."

Ebby stared into the water as Deni spoke hoping to catch a glimpse of Sofia, but she never saw anything other than a couple of small fish jumping out of the water. She decided to leave Slune the next morning and follow the river all the way to the Big Sea to find Sofia.

The day went by quickly, and their stomachs became sore from laughing so much. Nikola, Deni, and the other boys agreed to play together again the next morning.

Back at Nikola's house they had another delicious dinner before going to bed. This time Nikola put Ebby's pillow on his bed next to him. They talked about their amazing day. As Ebby began to fall asleep, Nikola held Ebby's face close to his. "Ebby, you are *magnificent*! Today was the best day of my life. I'm not sad anymore and I want you to live with me forever. You showed me and the other boys that our differences make us better together, not worse. We have more in common than any of us imagined and all it took was taking the time to get to know each other."

Ebby was touched by what Nikola said. "You are a sweet boy, Nikola, and you will make lots of friends. It would be fun to stay and play with you forever, but there is so much I want to see and do. I want to see where the sun goes at night and, more than anything, I want to find Sofia. If you're kind and helpful, you'll always have friends. I need to leave in the morning, but I know you can accomplish anything you want without me."

Nikola understood why Ebby wanted to leave; he just wished she did not have to go so soon. She had changed his life overnight just by being kind. They both fell asleep happier knowing they had a friend for life.

After another of Victoria's delicious breakfasts, Ebby started off on her next adventure to the Big Sea to find Sofia. Nikola headed off in the opposite direction to play Hide and Seek with his new friends. The boys were disappointed Ebby left Slune without saying goodbye. They ran after her, but she was already gone.

CHAPTER SIX

Among the Ruins

(In which Ebby tangles with a fox.)

Ebby left Slune following the same river that, by Deni's account, Sofia swam up from the Big Sea. The river zigzagged its way across The Land of Stones in a southwesterly direction. The farther she went from Slune, the flatter the land became until only a few hills dotted the horizon in front of her. She passed large groves of trees bearing strange shiny green and black balls. Red sleepy flowers covered the ground underneath the trees, which she avoided as her mother had told her to do.

Several hours later she spotted the remains of a big stone building on the top of a hill in the distance. Leaving the river bed she had been following, she set out towards the hill to investigate the building. She found a set of steps at the bottom of the hill and climbed up to the top.

Only a few of the walls of the building still stood, with the rest in piles on the ground. No one had lived in this place for a long time. She climbed over the piles of stones until she reached a hole in the wall where a window used to be. She jumped up on the ledge. The view was stunning. The building was on a cliff rising straight out of the Big Sea. Waves crashed against the rocks far below. She had never seen anything like this.

Ebby stood on the window ledge for several minutes watching the waves grow bigger and bigger before crashing against the rocks. She spotted a large town far away on the opposite side of the water. It was much bigger than Slune and she thought it should be her next destination. Suddenly, she saw a purple glistening figure rise briefly out of the water. She tried to focus on it, but it was gone as quickly as it had emerged. Her heart raced as she wondered if she had just seen Sofia, the purple sea dragon. She searched the surface of the water for a few more minutes then turned her attention back to the ruins.

For the first time that day, her tummy started growling from hunger. She leaped down from the window ledge and moved back towards the center of the ruins. The sound of the waves grew quieter, and she heard birds singing above her head. She scrounged around the ruins for something to eat, but all she came across was some dried tufts of grass growing between the fallen stones. She nibbled on a dull yellow blade of grass, but it was hard and flavorless. Nothing was delicious in these ruins, especially compared to the tasty treats Napoleon and Victoria had given her. She went back down the stairs to eat some grass and flowers in the field below.

The red sleepy flowers were beautiful, but she knew better than to eat them. She found some yummy yellow flowers

instead. As she nibbled happily on a flower, she detected a small reddish-brown creature with large pointy ears and a bushy red tail creeping up towards her from behind. It was not much bigger than she was. It had a long, pointed nose, and its lips were curled back exposing a set of bright white pointed teeth.

Ebby stopped mid-chew and sprang around. "Hi! I'm Ebby, who are..." Just as she was about to introduce herself, the reddish-brown fur ball pounced on her, nipping at her soft ear. Ebby squeaked with delight because the teeth were tiny and tickled her. She rolled around in the grass and flowers with the creature giggling so hard it stopped nibbling on her ear.

"Why are you laughing? Aren't you afraid of me?" the confused little reddish-brown ball of fur asked. "I'm a fox, and I'm supposed to eat bunnies. Aren't you a bunny?"

Ebby stopped giggling because the baby fox acted a little bit annoyed. "Yes, I'm a bunny. An Elusive Baby Bunny, to be exact. Why would I be afraid of you? You're little and friendly like me. Why would you want to eat a bunny? That sounds yucky. Wouldn't you rather eat some yummy yellow flowers and play with me instead?"

The fox tilted her head to one side as she thought about Ebby's questions. Eating a bunny did sound yucky! She had not eaten anything other than her mother's milk since she was born, but her mother told her she could not have milk forever. One day she would have to start eating bunnies. Today was definitely not the day to start eating bunnies she concluded after seeing Ebby's friendly smile.

"My name is Frisky. I live under the ruins with my mother, father, and older brother Rip. My brother teases me because I haven't eaten a bunny yet, even though he hasn't eaten one either. Rip and I were watching you in the ruins and then he dared me to eat you. You were supposed to be the first bunny I ever ate, and all I did was make you laugh. I'll never be a real fox." Frisky sat on her haunches and hung her head.

Ebby racked her brain for something to say that would cheer Frisky up. "Maybe you can be a different kind of fox. Maybe you can stand out in your own special way. Not every fox needs to eat bunnies, do they? Most bunnies stay close to home eating nothing but grass and flowers. I also eat bread, carrots, and berries. If I can be different, so can you. I can tell you're special. You just need to find your own way. Eating bunnies might work for Rip, but maybe you'll find there's more to life than eating bunnies."

Ebby's confidence and kindness, even after getting nibbled on, surprised Frisky. "Where are you going? Can I go with you?"

Ebby did not know exactly where she was going. She was following the sun, wanted to see the big town on the other side of the sea, and she wanted to find Sofia, the purple sea dragon. She thought it would be wonderful to have a friend exploring the world with her. "I am traveling the world to see everything there is to see and do everything there is to do. I would love for you to come with me but you need to check with your parents. I don't want them to worry about you."

"That sounds interesting," Frisky yipped excitedly, "and much better than sticking around here eating bunnies. Why don't you come meet my parents and we can ask them together."

Ebby agreed immediately and followed Frisky up the stairs to the ruins. While most bunnies would never agree to meet a family of foxes, Ebby was not most bunnies. She was an Elusive Baby Bunny. She was not afraid of anything because she knew kindness and a willingness to help was all anyone needed.

They went through an old broken-down doorway into a small room. In the corner of the room, underneath an old wooden door that had fallen off its hinges, was a dark hole leading to a tunnel under a pile of rocks. Ebby followed Frisky through the hole and into the tunnel. The light from the sun vanished, and Ebby found herself in complete darkness. She had not been in a burrow since she left home, so it took a few seconds for her eyes to adjust. At first all she could see were three pairs of yellow eyes staring at her. This must be Frisky's family, she thought to herself. Just as she was about to introduce herself, she heard a low growl rise directly below one of the sets of eyes.

CHAPTER SEVEN

Ebby in the Foxes' Den

(In which Ebby shows the true nature of her strength.)

Ignoring the low growl, and before any of the foxes could say or do anything, Ebby stood up on her back legs and introduced herself. "Hi. I'm Ebby, an Elusive Baby Bunny. I'm Frisky's new friend and it's super nice to meet you." As she said this, she dropped some yummy yellow flowers at their feet. All three sets of eyes blinked at once before turning to look at each other in stunned silence. Ebby's eyes adjusted to the darkness and she saw Frisky's parents and another baby fox who she assumed was Frisky's brother Rip.

Frisky's father was about to jump on Ebby, just like Frisky had done. But before he could pounce, Frisky's mother realized Ebby said she was an Elusive Baby Bunny. She raised her paw in front of Frisky's father and said, "Honey! That is no way to treat Frisky's new friend!"

Frisky's father stopped mid-pounce and sat down on his haunches, drool dripping off his tongue. Rip, who was also drooling, thought his mother was crazy. Never in the history of all Foxdom had a bunny marched directly into a fox den without getting immediately eaten. It was just not done. They were foxes. They were hungry, and she was a bunny. That's how it worked. End of story.

Ebby did not know that. She had never studied the history of Foxdom. All she knew was she needed to be polite, kind, and helpful when meeting new friends. So that is exactly what she did.

Frisky informed her family that Ebby was on a journey to explore the world and had invited Frisky to go with her. Frisky's mom and dad were stunned. All foxes grew up hearing stories about Elusive Baby Bunnies, but they certainly never expected to meet one. They were said to be so rare there was only one in the entire world at a time. Elusive Baby Bunnies reportedly had an unlimited capacity for kindness, bravery, and curiosity. They were also supposed to make exceptionally good things happen wherever they went.

Frisky's mother was not convinced Ebby was an Elusive Baby Bunny. Until she saw Ebby, Frisky's mom thought the stories were completely made up, just like stories about unicorns and dragons. "Tell us about where you came from and your adventures so far." Ebby told them her entire life story from growing up in Fluffle Valley to the moment she rolled around in the grass with Frisky. Frisky's father and Rip stopped drooling and listened intently as Ebby spoke. When Ebby finished, Frisky jumped up on her mom and dad and pleaded with them. "Can I please go with Ebby? Please?"

After hearing Ebby's story, Frisky's parents were certain Ebby was an Elusive Baby Bunny. Only an Elusive Baby Bunny would have been brave enough to leave her home and travel this far on her own. Further, only an Elusive Baby Bunny could have had such an extraordinary impact just by being kind. Even so, they were still nervous about letting Frisky go with Ebby. Frisky was their littlest pup, and she still only drank milk. The big town was far beyond where any fox from their family had ever gone. What if she got lost or hurt? What if they were not friendly on the other side of the Big Sea? What if Frisky never learned how to hunt bunnies? Would her life as a fox forever be changed? What would the other foxes say?

When the discussion slowed down, Ebby addressed Frisky's family. "I don't know anything about foxes. You're the first foxes I've met. And I don't know anything about the town on the other side of the sea because I've never been there. But a few days ago, I also didn't know you could see across Fluffle Valley just by standing on a log. The only thing I know for sure is it's been incredible to try new things and make new friends. None of that would have happened if I hadn't left my fluffle. I don't know if we will meet new friends on the other side of the Big Sea. I can only promise you I will be kind and helpful to everyone we meet. I promise to be Frisky's friend and to help her any way I can. I don't know if this will keep us safe, but I know I will do whatever I can for her, except let her eat me of course!"

Frisky immediately jumped in when Ebby had finished speaking. "Please, Mom. Please, Dad. Please let me go! I will never know what kind of fox I can be if I don't try different things. Just because no one in our family has ever traveled or made friends with a bunny doesn't mean it isn't worth trying."

Frisky's parents realized Ebby and Frisky were right. Kindness and the willingness to be helpful were powerful forces. Ebby literally walked into a fox den at dinnertime and won over an entire hungry fox family just by being kind! They felt confident Ebby would be an exceptional companion for Frisky. Frisky was being offered an opportunity to see and explore the world with an Elusive Baby Bunny. They knew this opportunity would never come again.

Frisky yipped gleefully as her dad said she could go with Ebby. She ran around the den nipping at Rip's tail. He, in turn, tried to stay away from his annoying little sister. When she was done tormenting her brother, she playfully jumped on Ebby again, this time licking her all over her face and ears. They rolled around like a big ball of laughing fur. They made up their minds to spend the rest of the day with Frisky's family and leave the next morning. Later, as Ebby and Frisky cuddled asleep together on a bed of dried leaves and grass, Frisky's parents watched their little bodies breathe in and out in complete peace. They were glad they had not eaten her.

CHAPTER EIGHT

The Lucky Rabbit Foot

(In which Ebby finds herself on the wrong end of a fox.)

Ebby woke up early the next morning. Frisky and her family were still asleep so she quietly left the den. Once she was beyond the ruins, she bounded down the stairs to the field of flowers below to eat breakfast. On the way there she felt one of her rear feet was a little wet. She thought it was strange but did not pay any more attention to it. She was hungry and started nibbling on some yummy flowers.

Without warning she heard something move directly behind her. Then, out of the corner of her eye, she saw a reddish-brown blur coming straight towards her. It was Rip. She felt a sharp sting as he nipped her rear foot. Rip was bigger than Frisky, and his teeth did not tickle Ebby like Frisky's teeth had. Stunned, Ebby froze and closed her eyes as tightly as she could. As quickly as it started, the tussle was over. Frisky and her parents leaped down the stairs to stand between Rip and Ebby.

Frisky was extremely upset with her brother. "Rip, how could you do that to Ebby? She's my friend!" Frisky waited for her parents to scold Rip, but they were not sure what to say.

Although they were disappointed in Rip, it was partly their fault. They spent a lot of time teaching Rip how to catch bunnies but apparently not enough time teaching Rip the value of friendship.

Frisky's father addressed Rip using his sternest voice. "Well, son, I guess we thought you knew how important Ebby was to Frisky and it would be enough to keep you from trying to eat her. I was just as surprised as you were when Frisky brought Ebby into our home and announced they were friends. My first instinct was to eat her too, but Ebby means a lot to Frisky. True friends like Ebby are more valuable than anything else in the world, and you have to protect them. We should have taught you it is not nice to eat your sister's friend, even if she happens to be a bunny. A good friend will help Frisky when she needs it most."

Rip hung his head low and stared at his white paws. He was embarrassed he had bitten Ebby. "I don't know why I did it. I just wanted to taste her. I've never eaten a bunny. I watched her sleep last night and tried to nibble on one of her feet, since she has four of them, just to get a taste. But I was afraid I would wake her up and thought it would be better to bite her while she ate breakfast. I wasn't going to eat all of her. I promise!"

It finally dawned on Ebby why one of her feet had been wet. She believed Rip did not mean to hurt her. She hopped around Frisky to stand in front of Rip. "I'm glad you didn't eat me, but I think I understand why you tried. You've been training to eat bunnies all your life. I came into your house, so of course you tried to eat me! I can't blame you for doing exactly what you were taught to do. If Frisky ate me yesterday our adventures would have ended before they even began.

Now we get to explore the world together! I know it's hard to go against your instincts and what you've been taught to do. But it can be great to try different experiences and learn new things. At least, that's what I am going to do."

Rip apologized to Ebby and asked her to forgive him, which she did immediately. She did not want Rip to feel bad, so she said, "You know, I have heard bunny feet bring bad luck, so it's probably a good thing you didn't eat one." The foxes all laughed when Ebby said this. Everyone in the Land of Stones had heard the old wives' tale that bunny feet were good luck charms. Ebby was living proof that the only bunny feet that brought good luck were the ones still attached to the bunny.

Frisky's mother stopped frowning at Rip and turned to Ebby. "You are really something special, Ebby. You're more than special. You are *magnificent*. Thank you for treating Rip so graciously and for being so understanding. We'll leave you to eat in peace and will send Frisky down to join you after her breakfast."

Rip led his parents back to their den with his tail tucked between his legs and his head still hanging in shame. Ebby assured Frisky she was fine, and Frisky ran after her family to eat breakfast and get ready to leave on their adventure.

A short time later, Frisky came back with Rip and her parents. Frisky's mother licked her face, cleaning off a drop of milk dangling from one of Frisky's whiskers. Although Frisky hated it when her mother licked her face, she did not turn away like she usually did. She knew her mother was worried about her leaving. Frisky took turns rubbing noses with each member of her family promising to be careful and come back when she had something worthwhile to tell them.

Ebby approached Rip, who had lingered behind his father. She touched her nose to his and smiled. Rip breathed a sigh of relief and smiled broadly back at her. Ebby knew she would never have to fear his sharp white teeth again. Frisky and Ebby headed off on their adventure to the big town on the other side of the Big Sea.

CHAPTER NINE

In the Company of Friends

*(In which Ebby and Frisky find their way with
the help of some new friends.)*

Bud Der's Farm

Ebby and Frisky walked along the seashore towards the town on the other side of the Big Sea. Sometimes they walked on rocks worn smooth by the constant motion of the waves. Other times the beach was covered with pebbles or fine grains of sand. Occasionally, when there was no shore to walk on, they climbed steep hills and walked along the cliff edge far above the water.

As they walked along the shore, they saw strange sea creatures with hard red and blue shells crawling sideways across the sand. Frisky tried to bite one to see what it was, but it pinched her nose with its claw and told her to back off. Frisky jumped in the air with a yelp and let it go. The crab scurried away sideways. After making sure Frisky was not hurt, Ebby mentioned how funny it was seeing the crab run sideways even though its eyes faced forward. They tried to do it themselves but got their feet tangled and they fell down laughing.

Ebby regularly scanned the surface of the water as she walked, hoping to see Sofia. She saw fish jumping in the sea and birds flying overhead, but she never saw the purple sea dragon. They came across big mounds of smelly seaweed and kelp washed ashore by the waves. Ebby tried to eat some of the leaves the first time she saw them, hoping they would be delicious. Instead, they tasted salty and bitter.

By the second day Ebby's stomach grumbled from hunger. There was plenty of grass growing close to the shore for Ebby to eat, but Frisky could not eat grass. Ebby did not want to eat in front of Frisky if Frisky did not have something to eat too. She wished she had some bread from Nikola's home, or a carrot, or some yummy yellow flowers to eat.

Frisky was hungry too. Her mother was always ready to feed her, but now she was far from home. The big town was still a day's journey away. Ebby was sure she would be able to find food for Frisky there but did not want Frisky to go another day without eating. "Let's go inland and see if we can find something for you to eat." Frisky agreed and they crossed through a field of grass and flowers.

After a short walk they came upon a big stone barn like the one on Napoleon's farm. A creature stood in front of the barn's open door looking out. He was almost as big as Napoleon but Ebby immediately realized he was not a horse because two sharp pointy spikes grew out of the top of his head. He leisurely chewed on dried grass while talking to a big white bird with something bright red on top of his head and below his chin. They stopped talking and stared with their mouths open at the unexpected sight of a baby fox and baby bunny walking up to them.

Ebby stood up on her back legs and said, "Hello. I'm Ebby and this is my friend Frisky. We've been walking for several days without anything to eat. This is Frisky's first time away from her mother, and she only knows how to drink milk. Do you have any milk you could give her? We would be grateful if you did."

The big creature smiled at Ebby and Frisky. "Yes, we have

plenty of milk and would be happy to give her some. We have enough for you too, if you're hungry." His voice was deep and friendly.

"Thank you so much," Ebby said with relief. "I promised her parents I would look after her." Frisky glanced over at Ebby and wagged her tail. Even though Frisky was the same age as her, Ebby had a sense of responsibility that went far beyond her age. It was comforting to Frisky knowing Ebby was watching out for her. "I don't need any milk for myself because I can eat flowers and grass from the field we passed. I apologize if I interrupted your conversation but I was so worried about her."

"You didn't interrupt our conversation at all," the big horned animal replied. He let a low laugh roll out from deep in his chest and shook his head. "We talk about the same old things all the time."

Making new friends and learning about them was one of Ebby's favorite things to do. "Do you mind telling us a little bit about you? You don't look anything like anyone we've met before."

"My name is Bud Der and I'm a bull," the big animal said. He pointed to the bird with his chin. "This little guy is my best friend, Racket. He's a rooster. Racket always claims he sees the sun before anyone else. Well, he definitely sees it before me! We were just talking about the noise he made this morning. He made a heck of a racket and woke me up, along with the rest of the farm—just like he does every morning! That's why we call him Racket." Bud winked at Ebby. "What about you, where are you from? And why is a baby bunny traveling with a fox? Now there's something you don't often see, isn't that right, Racket?"

Racket, who had been silently watching Bud and Ebby talk up to now, nodded his head, first up and down, then side to side trying to understand what he was witnessing. He had never met a fox up close and was curious how Frisky and Ebby ended up together. He had a couple of rooster friends who were last seen in the company of a fox, but his friends were never seen again after that. All they left behind were a couple of feathers. Racket always wondered what happened to them. They probably just went on an adventure together like Ebby and Frisky were doing, he concluded after seeing how well Ebby and Frisky got along. This made Racket feel better instantly.

Ebby and Frisky took turns telling Bud and Racket where they came from, how they met, and where they were going. When they finished telling Bud and Racket their stories, Bud asked Frisky. "Would you like to try some of my wife's milk?"

"Yes please," Frisky answered, wagging her tail eagerly.

"Everyone says my wife Ud Der has the best milk in the Land of Stones. Of course they also say her Bud Der is the sweetest." Bud let out a deep roll of chuckles, making his entire body shake. Racket shook his head as he tried to keep from cracking up.

"Bud is always making fun of their names. Bud Der and Ud Der! It never gets old."

Bud led Frisky into the barn where there was a big bucket of fresh milk on the ground. "Here you go, Frisky. Drink as much as you like. Whatever is left will go to the farmer's house." Frisky put her face close to the milk and started lapping it up with her tongue. It was warm, sweet, and rich. When she had her fill, she licked the milk from her whiskers.

"Thank you Bud, you were right! Your Ud Der's milk is

the best, and her Bud Der certainly is the sweetest!" Bud was impressed Frisky caught on to his joke so quickly.

Frisky and Bud Der went back outside to join Ebby and Racket, who were discussing who got up earlier in the morning. Racket enjoyed waking all his friends up the moment he saw the first rays of the sun. It brought him more pleasure than anything else in the world. Ebby woke up before the sun rose too, but she recognized how important it was for Racket to believe he was first to rise. She assured Racket he woke up before she did, which thrilled him. He practiced crowing for Ebby to show her how effective he was. Ebby covered her ears with her front paws as he screeched as loud as he could.

"You are the best crower I've ever heard." Ebby did not mention he was the only crower she had ever heard. Racket beamed, stuck out his chest, and strutted around the barnyard.

Bud smiled with relief as he heard Ebby compliment Racket. Racket paraded around the yard happier than he had been in a long time. For one thing, Racket was no longer worried about his missing friends. He imagined them having grand adventures like Ebby and Frisky. Then an Elusive Baby Bunny told him he was a great crower. A rooster could not get a higher compliment than that. As far as Racket was concerned, he had just been declared "The Best Crower in the Land of Stones." Bud hoped Racket might even sleep in the next morning so he could get a little extra rest. Bud, noticing Ebby had not eaten anything yet, offered Ebby some of his hay.

Ebby declined his offer, remembering the tasteless dried grass she ate at Frisky's ruins. "I saw some yummy yellow flowers on our way here. I'll eat some on our way back to the Big Sea. We still have a long way to go to get to the big town. Thank you for feeding Frisky. We'll never forget your kindness." Frisky nodded in agreement and licked her lips again for emphasis.

"Come back any time," Racket said as he puffed his chest out and strutted around the barnyard. "You can spend the night and sleep in the hen house. It's full of feathers and warm chickens. I'm certain it will be the softest, warmest place you will ever sleep. I'll happily wake you up in the morning." Frisky could not wait to tell her family about Racket's invitation to let her sleep in the hen house. She felt certain they would appreciate a soft bed made of feathers over the hard rocks they slept on back home.

As they headed to the coast, Ebby stopped along the way to eat her fill of flowers and grass. The sun was setting as they reached the cliff overlooking the sea. The sky's reflection on the water mirrored the colors in the sky. It was beautiful. Ebby pointed to the spot on the horizon where the sun was going down and said, "That's where we're going tomorrow." For a second, she thought she saw the waters ripple far off in the distance. She stared at the spot, hoping to see Sofia. Nothing happened. Full and tired from their journey, Ebby and Frisky curled up together and fell fast asleep under the bright stars.

CHAPTER TEN

The Artists' Colony

(In which Ebby and Frisky learn how to tap into their hearts.)

Ebby and Frisky woke early the next morning. They were too far from Bud Der's barn to hear Racket crowing, but Ebby was certain he was living up to his name.

The beach was full of tall white and grey birds walking back and forth along the beach. They pecked at the rocks and sand with their yellow beaks searching for something to eat. One bird found a small piece of food and screeched at his friends to come inspect it. Several birds flew over. As they stood around squawking about what a lovely piece of food it was, the first bird gulped it down right in front of them. The other birds walked away disappointed and renewed their hunt for food.

Ebby and Frisky watched this scene occur several times until something even stranger happened. As one of the birds bragged about the tasty morsel he found, one of the other birds grabbed it out from under him and flew away with it. All the other birds standing around burst out in a deafening noise and waved their wings wildly. The bird whose food was stolen pouted, but the rest of the birds laughed with amusement. Ebby did not understand this unusual behavior. She never ate in front of her friends if they were hungry, and she could not imagine stealing their food. These birds apparently enjoyed stealing each other's food because they did it repeatedly.

Ebby and Frisky watched the peculiar eating habits of the sea birds for a few more minutes before continuing their journey. Steep cliffs lined the shore as they walked down the beach. Soon the beach began to narrow until there was barely enough room for Ebby and Frisky to walk side by side. A short time later their path was blocked by a big rock jutting out into the sea. They either had to walk back and find a place to climb the cliffs or wade a short distance in the water to get around the rock. They agreed it would be quicker to reach the big town if they waded into the water.

First, Ebby tried getting around the rock on her own. A small wave came ashore and moved the sand beneath her feet. It nearly knocked her over. She steadied herself and braced for another wave. This wave was bigger and nearly covered her entire body with cold frothy water. She needed to walk on her back legs to keep her head above the water, but the waves and the soft sand made her too wobbly. Frisky was a little taller than Ebby and was able to walk into the waves on all four feet.

"Why don't you lean on me? We can go together," Frisky suggested.

Ebby stood on her back legs and put her front foot on Frisky's back to steady herself. They walked together into the water. Ebby discovered it was quite easy to keep her balance by holding onto Frisky. They safely waded around the rock in a few minutes and got back on dry land. Ebby knew she would not have been able to do it without Frisky's help. This reminded Ebby how much better it was to have friends than to be alone. They shook themselves dry and proceeded towards the town.

At first, there were only a few small houses scattered along the shore. As they neared the town, the number of houses grew and became closer together. Soon they found themselves in the center of the town. Most of the town was built on a hill and some buildings were quite tall. Narrow streets made of stone twisted their way up the hill between the buildings.

Small wooden boats were tied to the docks in front of the town. They rose and fell smoothly with the waves. A white and grey sea bird sat on top of a wooden post squawking to himself. Ebby and Frisky walked up to the bird and introduced themselves. This was all it took for him to tell them about the town and what he liked to eat. He spoke so fast they could barely keep up with him.

"I'm George C. Gull," he squawked. Without any additional encouragement from Ebby or Frisky he carried on. "Gulls live near the water and like anything we can find to eat, even if it belongs to someone else. In fact, we like it more if it belongs to someone else. It doesn't matter what it is: fish guts, pieces of garbage, bread, they're all delicious. Whenever I find something to eat, I like to tell all the gulls in town what I found before I eat it. This makes it taste better, especially if the other gulls want it. But do you know what my favorite thing is?"

Ebby thought back to the scene on the beach when they watched the birds. "When it belongs to someone else?"

"Exactly! The absolute *best* tasting food is anything I can steal from another gull while he's telling me how good it's going to be. There's nothing better. Nothing. Well, there is one thing better, stealing from someone bigger than me. But that's hard to do."

Ebby and Frisky finally understood what the birds they saw earlier in the morning were doing. After telling them about gull eating habits, George C. Gull told them about the town.

"It's called Roveen. The ancient humans built it a thousand years ago." Ebby did not quite know how long a thousand years was but she assumed the town was older than her parents.

"Some of the people who live in Roveen are fishermen. They row their boats far out to sea to catch fish. Gulls love fishermen because they always have lots of fish guts for us. Sometimes a smart gull like me can steal a whole fish if he's fast enough." George stuck his chest out proudly. "I've only done it once, but it was the best thing I ever ate. The man was ten times bigger than me and boy did he get angry. Nothing tasted as scrumptious as that fish!" Just thinking about it made George hungry all over again but that did not stop him from talking.

"Roveen is also full of artists who spend their time making beautiful things. Some use bright colors to make paintings.

Some make things out of clay, seashells, or rocks. Others write stories on paper. Artists are nice, but they don't have fish guts like the fishermen. They just have a lot of old stale bread. I'm pretty sure that's all they eat."

Ebby and Frisky politely listened to George as he talked, but after the fifth food story they were ready to see Roveen for themselves and maybe find something to eat. All his talk about food was making them hungry. When George finally paused to catch his breath, Ebby jumped at the chance. "Thank you for all the information about gulls and Roveen. You're helpful and obviously know a lot. I promise if I find anything tasty, I'll bring it to you."

George shook his head. "It wouldn't taste good if you gave it to me," he said. "It's only tasty if you don't want me to eat it!" Ebby and Frisky laughed as they left George and headed towards the center of town. He was still chattering with himself as they walked away.

They turned onto the first street they found. The cobblestones had been worn smooth over the centuries and fit together like a jigsaw puzzle. The doors and windows in the buildings were all closed and no one was on the street. "It's still early," Frisky whispered to Ebby. "They're probably still asleep." The street was narrow and sloped upwards, snaking its way between the buildings.

"We might be able to see the entire town if we get to the highest point," Ebby said indicating uphill.

Some buildings were new and brightly colored. Others were old and broken down like the ruins where Frisky lived. At the end of the road near the top of the hill, they found a small park with a bench and an old stone wall. A small furry black animal with a long tail sat on top of the wall. He licked his paws, pretending to ignore Ebby and Frisky as they approached. The black animal stopped licking his paws and turned his attention to the strange little pair standing in front of him. His eyes were green and the tip of his tail moved about gracefully as if it had a mind of its own. Ebby and Frisky had never seen a creature like him before and Ebby wanted to know all she could about him. Ebby walked up to the wall and stood as tall as she could and, after introducing herself and Frisky, asked him what he was.

"Hello, I'm Miko. I'm a cat," the furry black animal said. Miko had never seen a bunny or a fox in Roveen before but hoped they would be satisfied with his reponse and leave him alone in peace.

"Do you live here?" Ebby asked.

Miko, realizing he was not going to get rid of them so

quickly, spoke to them again. "I live with a human family, but I prefer to be left alone unless I'm hungry. Sometimes I let them rub my stomach if I don't have anything better to do. You'll find humans get great pleasure from petting small, soft, furry animals." He watched Ebby and Frisky exchange a puzzled look. "I know, I don't get it either but if it makes them happy, and they keep giving me food, I don't mind it much." Miko yawned a lot and kept circling around on top of the wall as if he was searching for something. Although he was polite, Miko did not want to spend any more time with Ebby and Frisky than necessary.

"Did you lose something?" Ebby asked, glancing at the ground under the wall to see if she could help Miko find whatever he lost.

"No, I'm just looking for the ideal place to take a nap. I always take a long nap in the sun after I've finished my morning bowl of milk."

"Do you have any milk you could share with Frisky?" Ebby asked hopefully.

"No, I'm sorry, I don't. I didn't expect to have visitors this early in the morning, let alone a hungry fox and a baby bunny. Some people leave bowls of milk outside their front doors for hungry cats. I'm sure you'll find a bowl on the way to where ever you're going." Miko turned around one more time and lay down. He stretched his front paws before curling up on the wall and closing his eyes. The tip of his tail twitched a few more times before settling down. Moments later he was sound asleep.

Since they were so close to the top of the hill, Ebby and Frisky climbed the stone wall behind the park. They scrambled up a pile of rocks and then jumped onto the wall. Balancing carefully, they walked to the end of the wall and looked down at the town. They could see all the way to the docks where they met George and beyond to the edge of the sea. They felt like they were on the top of the world.

They could tell it would be difficult finding their way around town. The buildings faced different directions, and the little narrow streets went every which way. They agreed it would be fun to wander through the streets. Ebby loved to explore new places because she never knew what she might find. As an Elusive Baby Bunny, others might not know where she was, but she always knew she was just where she needed to be.

They jumped off the wall and headed down a narrow street

going in the opposite direction from where they met Miko. Windows and doors started opening as the townspeople began pouring into the streets to begin their day. After almost getting run over by a woman carrying a basket full of fresh bread for sale, they turned off onto a smaller, quieter street.

The street they picked was narrow and dark. The sun never made its way to the ground here. The buildings were old and appeared ready to fall over. Grass and weeds grew between the cobblestones in the street. Just when Ebby thought they should go back to the bigger street an old wooden door opened and a small man stepped outside.

His clothes were old and covered with bright splotches of color. A black and white beard hung down to the middle of his stomach. As he bent over to place a bowl of fresh milk on the street the tip of his beard fell into it. He wiped the milk from his beard as he stood up and rubbed his hand on his pants. He was about to go back through the door when he spotted Ebby and Frisky staring up at him. His face broke into a huge smile before offering the bowl of milk to them. Frisky ran to the bowl of milk and started lapping it up. It was delicious and tasted like Ud Der's milk.

Ebby, meanwhile, stood up to introduce herself. "Hello, I'm Ebby. Thank you for giving Frisky some milk. We haven't eaten since yesterday. Roveen is so welcoming. Our friend George C. Gull told us about the people who live in Roveen. Are you an artist or a fisherman?"

"Hello, my friends," the bearded man said, beaming with happiness. "My name is Soto. I am an artist. I used to be a fisherman when I was younger, but I like painting much more than fishing. What are you doing in Roveen? It's unusual to see a bunny and a fox traveling together. Have you traveled far?"

Ebby explained that she came from Fluffle Valley and how she had met Frisky along the way. "I've come a long way, but there is so much more I want to see and do. I've just begun my journey."

Soto was astonished. "You sound like an Elusive Baby Bunny! Are you one?"

"Yes, I am. You've heard of Elusive Baby Bunnies before?"

"Of course I have! Almost everyone has heard of Elusive Baby Bunnies! Some think you are imaginary, but I have always known you are real. This is truly extraordinary! You are the second Elusive Baby Bunny I've met in my life! The other one was a long time ago when I was traveling far away from Roveen in a place called the Land of Dragons. Most people live their entire lives never seeing a single Elusive Baby Bunny, but now I've met two! I am truly honored." Ebby was intrigued that Soto had met another Elusive Baby Bunny. She wondered if he had met Rebby the Gallant. Soto interrupted Ebby's train of thought before she could ask him about Rebby.

"Would you like to see my art studio?" Ebby nodded her head enthusiastically and wiggled her tail. She followed Soto into his studio while Frisky finished drinking the bowl of milk. It was dark and cool inside. The ceiling was not much higher than Soto's head. The walls and floor were cluttered with beautiful paintings.

"I love working with color and light and creating paintings for my friends to enjoy," he said as he pointed to several of his paintings. Some of them were of Roveen's street scenes, including places Ebby recognized from her walk to the top of the hill. Big waves crashed against the cliffs in one painting, while another showed fishermen and their boats painted in intricate detail.

A painting Soto had recently finished was drying on an easel in the back corner of the studio. It was a painting of three pieces of green fruit. On a shelf next to the painting were the three pears in the painting. "Would you like one of the pears? I've finished painting them and you must be hungry too." Soto pointed to where Frisky was lapping up the milk.

"Yes, thank you! I've never had a pear before and would love to try one." Soto placed the largest one on the ground next to her. She sniffed the fruit before taking a big bite. Sweet juice ran down her chin. "It's delicious! I've never tasted anything quite like this before."

As Ebby ate the pear, Frisky came into the studio to see Soto's artwork. Like Ebby, Frisky had never seen a painting before. Soto's paintings were extremely detailed and lifelike. Soto held up a painting of a rooster, which reminded her of

Racket. It was so realistic that Frisky thought she saw it move. Frisky imagined it could wake Soto up every morning if it wanted. She moved back and forth in front of the painting and was convinced the eyes followed her. She sniffed the painting to see if it smelled like Racket, but there was no odor.

Soto noticed Frisky's interest in the rooster painting and showed them a selection of other animals he had painted. "It's a passion of mine to paint all the creatures from the Land of Stones."

"How did you learn to paint?"

Soto smiled at Frisky and rubbed his beard thoughtfully. "I don't know exactly. I was a fisherman when I was younger, like my father, and his father before him. I worked on my father's fishing boat for many years but always dreamed of doing something different. At night I would stay awake late and draw pictures of the things I had seen during the day. One day I met an old artist who was painting a picture of the sea. The painting was so realistic and colorful it made me feel like I was in the picture.

"I decided at that moment I didn't want to be a fisherman anymore. I wanted to become an artist. I have been painting since that day. I still go fishing with my father sometimes, but I am no longer a fisherman."

Frisky thought she knew exactly how Soto felt. She came from a long line of bunny-eating foxes. She broke away from being a bunny-eater like her family, just as Soto had decided against being a fisherman. It was hard to do something different, but she saw how satisfied Soto was doing what he liked to do. "How can I become an artist? Can you teach me how to be a painter?"

Soto smiled and rubbed his fingers through his beard again as he thought about how to answer her questions. Finally, he said, "I cannot teach you how to be a painter, although there are others who can. For me, you must feel it. If you want to become a painter, pick up a paintbrush and paint from your heart."

Ebby listened to Frisky and Soto talk as she ate her pear. His advice was simple. To do the thing you love, you just have to start doing it.

CHAPTER ELEVEN

Soto Offers Frisky Guidance

(In which Frisky learns how to choose her own path.)

Soto spent the rest of the day showing Ebby and Frisky around Roveen. Soto introduced them to several of his friends who were artists. They loved what they created and gladly showed Ebby and Frisky how they made their beautiful paintings, sculptures, jewelry, fabric, and pottery. Ebby and Frisky did not meet any fishermen because they were already out fishing on their boats.

Ebby watched Frisky with pleasure as they met the artists of Roveen. Ebby already knew what she wanted to do. She was an Elusive Baby Bunny. She wanted to see and do everything. Frisky, however, was just beginning to discover her possibilities.

As the day went on, Frisky's head filled with thoughts about becoming the first fox painter in the Land of Stones. She told Soto her idea. Later that day when they were back in his studio he gave Frisky a small canvas and a set of paints. "All right, Frisky, now paint from your heart!"

Frisky stared at the little canvas, then at the paints, then back at the canvas. Each time she did this, the canvas appeared to get larger. Finally she dipped the end of her tail into the paint and closed her eyes, concentrating as hard as she could on her heart. She wanted to paint Ebby. The harder she tried to concentrate the faster her heart beat. She opened her eyes. Soto smiled reassuringly. He knew how hard it was to do something for the first time.

"Go ahead. Just try," he said. "The only bad thing that can happen is to never try and never know whether you were a painter in your heart. Maybe your heart will tell you to do something different, but you will never know unless you give it a chance."

Frisky moved her tail across the canvas. She tried brown paint first, then yellow, red, and green. Each time she added a new color, the painting got worse. It was a blurry mess. Soto watched her in silence as she struggled with the painting. After a few minutes Frisky stopped and sighed. It was hard work to paint something beautiful like Soto. Turning to him, she said, "I tried to paint from my heart, but my tail didn't want to listen! This doesn't look anything like what I told my heart to paint!"

Soto patted Frisky's head reassuringly. "Frisky, it takes time and patience to become good at anything. The heart is merely one tool to help you choose what you want to do. You need to learn some things at school. You can learn other things naturally. It's different for everyone. You're young and have time to choose what you want to do. In the meantime, don't be afraid to try lots of different things.

"I've painted for a long time. I wasn't always good. The first time I picked up a paintbrush was awful. But I knew in my heart I wanted to be a painter, so I practiced until I became better. I talked to other artists and watched them paint. I read books about artists who lived long ago and saw what they created. Each time I learned more about art I knew I wanted to be a painter. There were times when I thought I would never get better, but my heart always told me to keep trying. Eventually I got better.

"The artists you met today have worked on their skills for a long time. None were experts the first time they tried. Many did different things before they found what they liked to do. Some were fishermen, house builders, or farmers. If you love what you do, your heart will sing for you."

Frisky listened closely to Soto's words. She resolved right then to always listen to her heart.

CHAPTER TWELVE

The Painting Shack

(In which Ebby and Frisky discuss their futures.)

After cleaning Frisky's tail as best as he could, Soto invited them to stay at his farm in the countryside. He led them on a short walk to a stone house built in the middle of a grove of old twisted trees outside of Roveen. The trees were full of the same small black and green fruits growing near Frisky's home. "Those are olives," Soto told them after noticing Ebby sniffing one that had fallen.

The ground between the trees was covered with tall green grass, yummy yellow flowers, and sweet smelling purple flowers. "When I'm not painting, I like working in my garden," Soto explained. "I grow carrots, potatoes, onions, cabbage, and other fruits and vegetables. It's rewarding to eat something you have grown yourself. I enjoy being in Roveen with the other artists, but I enjoy nature even more."

The farm was warm and cozy, unlike the dark alley where they met Soto. Soto pulled a couple of carrots from his garden for Ebby and set a bowl of milk down for Frisky. Ebby thanked him for what he had shown them, for all that he had taught them, and for bringing them into his home. "What can we do to repay your kindness?" Ebby asked.

Soto rubbed his beard. "More than anything, the one thing I would like to do is paint you both. Bunnies and foxes sometimes come into my yard, but they run away when they see me. The first Elusive Baby Bunny I met departed before I could paint him. Would you let me paint you?"

Ebby remembered Soto saying it was his passion to paint all the creatures from the Land of Stones. She and Frisky were honored Soto wanted to paint them. "Will you use your beard to paint me?" Frisky jokingly asked him because she had used her tail to paint Ebby.

He winked at Frisky. "I think it'll turn out better if I use a paint brush and paint with my fingers. My beard is even messier than your tail."

That night Ebby and Frisky slept outside. They found the same stars in the sky that shone above their homes far away. They talked about all the things they saw in Roveen. "Do you like painting?" Ebby asked Frisky.

"It seemed easy and magical when Soto was doing it, but I'm not sure painting is for me." Frisky admitted. "I enjoy being on this journey with you, making friends, and learning about the Land of Stones. I keep thinking about my family back home, wishing I could share our adventures with them. They will probably never leave home to visit Roveen on their own." Frisky wondered if there was something she could do. "What do you want to do, Ebby?"

Ebby stared up at the moon and stars above her and said, "I am an Elusive Baby Bunny. I want to see everything there is to see and do everything there is to do." They fell asleep curled up together in a ball as the stars twinkled above them.

The next morning after eating breakfast, Soto found a nice spot in the grass for Frisky to sit while he painted her. "Painting Frisky is going to take a while," he said to Ebby as he prepared his canvas, paints, and brushes. "I know how much Elusive Baby Bunnies like to explore, feel free to look around the farm if you want." Soto sat down.

Ebby was curious to see how Soto painted and stayed to watch him for a bit before wandering around the olive grove.

Soto dabbed his brush into different colors on his palette and applied the paint to the canvas. After a few minutes she watched in amazement as Frisky's eyes popped out of the canvas. "The eyes are the most important part of the painting," Soto advised Ebby. "If you can capture the eyes, the rest of the painting falls into place." Ebby left to wander around the farm while he began painting Frisky's nose.

Ebby started in the garden. She looked around the yard as she nibbled on a couple of yummy yellow flowers growing between the carrot tops. In the far corner of the yard, hidden from the house behind a row of large olive trees, Ebby discovered a small wooden shack with a large metal lock on the door. The windows were too high for her to see through. She was about to go back to watch Soto paint Frisky when he came walking towards her.

"Hello, Ebby, I thought I might find you back here. I need a few more brushes and paints from my studio. Would you like to go inside?"

"Yes, please," she said without delay. She sensed there was something interesting inside since there was such a big lock on such a small door. Ebby watched as Soto pulled an old rusty metal key out of his pocket.

"Sometimes I paint here when I don't feel like going to town." He jiggled the key in the lock until the key turned. "I think you'll like some of the paintings." The door hinges screeched as if they had not been used for a long time.

"This is my most special place. I have never let anyone else in here. You, however, are an Elusive Baby Bunny, and I think you should come inside."

The shack was surprisingly bright and airy. The windows and open door let the sun in. A fine dust coated the floor, which they disturbed when they walked in. The walls and floors were covered with Soto's paintings. An easel stood next to the window, and a partially finished painting rested on it. The painting was of a purple sea dragon.

CHAPTER THIRTEEN

Sofia, the Purple Sea Dragon

(In which Ebby learns the history of the Purple Sea Dragon.)

Ebby stood staring at the half-finished painting. She felt her heart race. Soto had finished painting the purple sea dragon's eyes and had started painting her long glistening body, which was partially covered by turquoise blue water. Her eyes were striking. There were glints of gold, blue, pink, and purple in them as if they held the glow of the most beautiful sunset. Soto busily grabbed some paints and brushes to take back to Frisky. "That's Sofia," he said as he left Ebby to explore the shack on her own. "I think the two of you should meet."

Ebby turned towards the paintings on the walls. Some were of fruits and vegetables from his garden or landscapes of Roveen, but most of them were of Sofia. He had painted her at several locations and at different stages in her life. In one, she stood in the waves near the shore. In others she swam undersea or flew over the mountains. There were many more paintings of Sofia in various stages of completion stacked on the floor. Ebby lost track of time studying Soto's paintings. She may have actually seen Sofia. She did exist!

Ebby's train of thought was broken when Frisky ran to the shack to invite Ebby to dinner. Before Ebby could mention Sofia or show Frisky Soto's paintings of her, Frisky gushed out that Soto promised to introduce her to Ivan LeKar, a famous author who lived in Roveen. She could not believe her good fortune to discover there was a way to share her adventures with her family that did not involve dipping her tail in paint. Frisky flicked her tail nimbly from side to side for emphasis as she told Ebby her tremendous news. Ebby did not want to detract from Frisky's excitement by mentioning Sofia. This was Frisky's time to shine, and Ebby let her talk uninterrupted all the way back to the house.

Soto came out of the house carrying a big piece of dried cheese, bread, olive oil, and a bowl of olives. He sat down at a low table under an olive tree where a bowl of milk and some carrots already waited for them. Soto broke off some bread and a chunk of cheese. A few crumbs fell into his beard and jiggled around as he chewed. George C. Gull had been right about artists eating bread, Ebby thought to herself, smiling. She nibbled silently on a carrot until she thought she was going to burst. When she could no longer stay quiet, she said, "Please, Soto, tell me about Sofia!" Soto's eyes sparkled with glee. He told Ebby to eat her dinner and he would tell her about the purple sea dragon.

Soto lowered his voice to make sure no one could overhear him and leaned closer to Ebby and Frisky before beginning to speak. "Sofia was born on an island far to the north of the Land of Stones in the Land of Dragons. During the first year of her life, she played all day with her friends, practicing all the things important for a dragon to know. They chased other sea creatures and practiced diving to the bottom of the sea to see how long they could hold their breath. She did this every day for a year, and every day she saw her grandfather, Seamus, sitting alone staring at small pools of water among the rocks on the shore.

"One day as Sofia was heading out to the deep water to play with her friends, a teardrop fell from her grandfather's eye as he was sitting on the shore. Since a dragon's tear instantly turns into a diamond, it made a big splash when it hit the water. Sofia had a kind heart and did not want to see her grandfather cry. She told her friends to play without her and went to speak to her grandfather." Ebby was relieved to hear that Sofia did not like to see her grandfather sad. Nothing made Ebby feel worse than to see someone suffering.

"Sofia asked her grandfather why he was sad. He told her he was not crying because he was sad, but because watching her play with her friends reminded him of what he was like when he was her age. It made him think back over his own life with fondness and think about the wonderful experiences Sofia still had in front of her.

"Sofia asked why he spent his days staring out at the sea. 'I am not looking out at the sea,' he told her. 'I'm looking *into* it.'" Soto paused for a moment for Ebby to appreciate the importance of Seamus' words.

"Seamus asked Sofia to sit next to him and examine the tide pool at his feet. He explained to her that tide pools were created each day when the tide went out. New water flowed in, and the old water was washed out each time the tide changed. Sofia already knew this, and there was nothing special about them as far as she could tell. On occasion she would jump into one, splashing water all over. She didn't think there was any reason to stare at them all day long like her grandfather did, but she did as he asked and stared at the pool.

"At first, Sofia could only see her reflection floating on the surface of the water. Seamus could tell that Sofia didn't understand what he was asking her to do and told her to look below the surface. She peered into the clear water at her feet. Sofia focused her eyes below the surface of the water and down into the depths of the pool. Soon she observed small fish, crabs, starfish, jelly fish, and a variety of water plants. There was an entire world living right under her nose." Ebby gasped. She had walked past lots of pools on the beach on the way to Roveen and had not paid any attention to them. She wondered how many tiny worlds she missed.

Soto continued, "When he was young, Seamus had traveled the world hoping to see everything there was to see. He flew to the tops of the highest mountains and swam to the bottom of the deepest oceans. Most of the time he was alone, but he never got tired of having new experiences and seeing new things. That is, until he met Sofia's grandmother and fell madly in love with her. Soon they had children, and Seamus promised her he would not travel around the world anymore.

"At first Seamus was sad there were parts of the world he hadn't seen. He'd heard of a place called The Land of Stones where there was a town built on top of rivers and waterfalls. He heard of another land near the bottom of the world where there were strange creatures unlike anywhere else. Instead of going on his own adventures he watched his children grow and explore the world. This filled his heart with a different kind of happiness. Now, watching Sofia grow up in front of him, he thought she might have the biggest adventures yet. This is what brought a tear to his eye. In the meantime, there was an entire unexplored world at his feet he could visit daily and still be home for dinner.

"Sofia listened as her grandfather pointed to the different forms of sea life at their feet, and she imagined it as a tiny version of her own world. From that day on, Sofia spent as many days with her grandfather learning about his travels around the world as she did playing in the water with her friends honing her dragon skills. Seamus made her promise that when she learned how to fly she would explore the world far away as well as the world at her feet. Both worlds, he emphasized, were important to know.

"When Sofia grew older and was able to leave her home to see the world, the first place she went was to the Land of Stones to see the village built entirely on rivers and waterfalls." Ebby immediately recognized the town.

"Slune!" she yelled out.

"Exactly!" Soto replied. "Sofia did not have a good experience in Slune but never told me what happened." Ebby wondered if it had something to do with the way the villagers ran away from her when she arrived.

Soto then shared with them the first time he saw Sofia. "It was a hot day so I went for a swim in the Big Sea. I swam a short distance from the shore where the sea is deeper and cooler. The water was as clear as glass and I saw a large colorful shell on the sea floor. I thought it would be challenging to paint. As I was getting ready to dive down to retrieve it, I saw a large glistening purple creature swimming below me. At first, I was alarmed and started to swim quickly to the shore. I expected the creature to chase me, but instead it dove to the sea floor and retrieved the shell. I watched in amazement as the purple creature moved in my direction until it was only a few feet away. I thought I was about to get eaten, when the most beautiful creature imaginable rose to the surface and held out the shell for me to take. As soon as I saw Sofia's eyes, I knew I had nothing to fear."

Soto took a bite of cheese and stared blankly at the sky, lost in thought for a moment as he remembered the first time he saw her. He had been trying to capture her eyes perfectly in his paintings ever since. Ebby saw that Soto's mind had wandered and cleared her throat gently to get Soto's attention so he would finish his story. He shrugged his shoulders apologetically.

"I'm sorry. It's easy for me to get lost in Sofia's eyes. Where was I? Ah, yes, I asked her to have lunch with me. She was surprised because she had never been so warmly greeted by a human before. She told me that most humans ran away from her when they saw her, which hurt her terribly. After our first lunch together she visited me often and I painted her many times. I have kept her a secret all these years and carefully locked my paintings in my studio until now because very few are ready to meet a dragon."

CHAPTER FOURTEEN

Ebby and Sofia

(In which Ebby meets Sofia and learns they have much in common.)

Ebby was spellbound listening to Soto's story about Sofia. "I have seen her!" Ebby exclaimed. "I only saw a glimpse of her from far away, but I know it was her!" She told Soto about the purple flashes she saw in the Big Sea. Since Frisky had not seen Soto's paintings of Sofia, Soto led them back to his studio for her to see them.

It was difficult for the three friends to sleep that night. Ebby could not stop thinking about meeting Sofia and the adventures they could have together. Sofia sounded just like an Elusive Baby Bunny. Frisky could not stop thinking about meeting the famous writer, Ivan LeKar. She imagined how fun it would be to write about her experiences and share them with her family and friends back home. And Soto could not wait to finish painting Frisky and start painting Ebby. He would be the first artist to ever paint an Elusive Baby Bunny. The stars sparkled overhead as they tossed and turned.

For the first time in her life, Ebby thought the sun rose far too early the next morning. She was just falling asleep when the first sunrays poked through the olive trees. Frisky had slept soundly and woke up eager for Soto to finish her painting so he could introduce her to Ivan LeKar. Soto had already finished breakfast and was getting his brushes ready when Frisky joined him. They let Ebby sleep a little longer, which was not at all normal for an Elusive Baby Bunny.

When Ebby woke up, it was nearly midday and Soto was putting his final strokes on the painting. Ebby made it just in time to see him add the last whisker. "What do you think?" he asked her before showing it to Frisky.

"It's a masterpiece!"

Soto had captured Frisky's soft fur, sparkly eyes, and sweet smile perfectly. He even added a few yummy yellow flowers to show how big she was in comparison.

Frisky, who had been sitting still for what felt like a life-time, ran over to the portrait. She had never seen herself before. "Is that what I look like?" Ebby and Soto nodded their heads in unison. "I look just like Rip!" She wagged her tail and licked Soto's hand in appreciation.

Soto wanted to paint Ebby next but he knew enough about Elusive Baby Bunnies to know she would not be able to sit still for long. She wanted to meet Sofia, and he did not want to be the reason their meeting was delayed. "Would you rather sit for your portrait now or meet Sofia?" he asked with a grin, fully knowing the answer.

"Please, can we meet Sofia?" Ebby pleaded. "I promise I will let you paint me afterwards."

"Of course," Soto replied, jumping to his feet. "Let's go find her!" Soto put Frisky's painting in a safe place to dry, and the three of them started down a path to the sea. They passed an old gnarled tree growing close to the path. There was a big hole in the base of the trunk.

Soto reached down into the hole and retrieved a tiny bell and hammer wrapped in a purple cloth. They both fit easily into the palm of his hand and appeared to be made of glass.

"Sofia gave me this bell and hammer many years ago to con-tact her. They're made entirely of dragon diamonds. No one but me can use them to call her. Somehow the bell senses my love for Sofia and magically uses that love to send a message to her, regardless of where she is. I've rarely used it because she's usually exploring the far reaches of the world. However, since Ebby thinks she saw Sofia swimming in the Big Sea, she may be in the Land of Stones and I know she'll want to meet you."

He folded the purple cloth neatly and placed it back inside

the hole. He carried the diamond bell and hammer to the shore. Once they were at the water's edge, Soto hit the bell with the hammer. The air filled with a beautiful sound, which oddly smelled of flowers. Ebby had never experienced anything like it before. She anxiously focused on the water, hoping to see Sofia. Nothing happened. Soto reassured her, "Be patient, little one. She will come as soon as the sound reaches her ears."

The strange musical note played continuously even though Soto only hit the bell once. Soto and Frisky sat on a flat rock to wait. Ebby stood at the edge of the water, never taking her eyes off the sea. After a few minutes the surface of the water became choppy. Waves rushed up on the shore, getting her feet wet. Soto and Frisky leaped up and hurried over to stand next to Ebby. A large purple body moved quickly under the water towards them. Before Ebby had time to move out of the way, Sofia burst out of the water and landed a few feet from Soto and his stunned friends.

Sofia was three times bigger than Napoleon and Bud Der, who were the biggest creatures Ebby had ever seen.

This made Sofia many times bigger than Ebby. Her skin was completely smooth and sparkled like gold. She was purple, but at the same time, she was blue, green, and pink, depending on where the sun hit her. Her eyes were as stunning as in Soto's paintings, like the bluest sky and the most colorful sunset all at once. She had a row of large bright white teeth, but they did not frighten Ebby. Instead, they reminded her of Frisky's teeth, which tickled her the first time they met. There was nothing scary about them. Sofia opened her wings and shook them, throwing water everywhere.

"I'm so sorry for getting you wet," she said in a voice that sounded like Soto's bell. It made Ebby think of flowers and happiness. "I was on my way to explore an old ship I found deep in the water near one of the Stone Islands when I heard the bell. I swam here as fast as I could."

Soto introduced Sofia to Ebby and Frisky. Sofia immediately recognized that Ebby was an Elusive Baby Bunny. "My grandfather, Seamus, told me about an Elusive Baby Bunny he met many years ago named Rebby. He was the same Elusive Baby Bunny Soto met. What a strange and wonderful coincidence! There are not many of you in the history of the world and I am so honored to meet you, Ebby."

Ebby couldn't believe Sofia had heard about Elusive Baby Bunnies!

"Let's go back home and relax a bit," Soto suggested. As they walked back to Soto's house, they stopped to return the bell and hammer to the tree on the path. "Are you hungry?" Soto asked Sofia. She shook her head. "Well, there's plenty of food here if you change your mind," Soto replied, pointing at the hole in the tree. Ebby and Frisky were curious about the hole, but did not say anything. They all sat down in the shade of his olive orchard.

They talked for hours, getting to know one another. Sofia told them about her recent adventures to the land of the strange creatures in the south. She saw giraffes with necks as long as a tall tree, hippopotamuses with enormous tusks who lived almost their entire lives in the water even though they were not sea creatures, and elephants who had large floppy ears and long trunks where their noses should be.

"One of the best things about making new friends from

different parts of the world," Sofia said, "is discovering our differences. But when you get to know each other, you can see how much we have in common. We may appear to be different at first, but we share the same dreams. We all want to be happy and loved."

Ebby remembered her conversation with Nikola. "My friend Nikola was just like the other boys in Slune but they treated him differently because he was from a different village."

Sofia sighed, "Sometimes the unusual one is the one most in need of love and friends. I've seen that happen many times before and I know how Nikola felt. I'm often the one everyone fears. It's hard making friends when you're a dragon, but I will never stop trying."

"Nikola wanted to see a purple sea dragon; it's all he talked about," Ebby said. "Were you the dragon that visited Slune?"

Sofia took a deep breath. "Slune was the first place I visited when I left the Land of the Dragons. My grandfather had heard of this mystical village built on rivers and waterfalls and wanted me to tell him what it was like. When I approached the dock to greet the villagers they screamed and ran away. I felt so lonely and unwelcome. I still feel horrible about it. I wish I could do something to let them know they don't need to be afraid of me, but I don't know how I could ever go back there without scaring them again.

"What's worse is that I never told my grandfather what happened because I'm so ashamed. He thinks I don't want to go there, but I just want a chance to go back and have a good story to tell him. I feel awful not telling him the truth."

After a little more discussion, Soto realized he was late taking Frisky to meet Ivan LeKar. "I need to take Frisky to Roveen.

Please excuse us for leaving so soon, but we can meet back here later for dinner. I can see you have much to talk about."

Sofia asked Ebby to tell her how she ended up in Roveen with Soto. Ebby explained how she stood on a log and saw the world beyond her fluffle for the first time. Once she discovered the outside world, she wanted to explore it. Her path to Roveen and Soto was somewhat by chance, but reflecting back on it, it was exactly what she was supposed to do.

Ebby described her journey to Roveen and the friends she made along the way. Sofia was affected by Ebby's description of Napoleon and how he longed to hear the wind singing in his ears again. When Ebby reached her encounter with the gulls on the beach and George's explanation of gull eating etiquette, Sofia laughed so hard small diamond tears fell from her eyes. She had always wondered why gulls made so much noise when they ate. It finally made sense.

Ebby concluded, "I promised George if I found something tasty, I would give it to him. But he told me it wouldn't be delicious unless I want to keep it for myself. I feel horrible because I don't know how I'm going to be able to keep my promise."

"I have an idea," Sofia said with a toothy grin.

CHAPTER FIFTEEN

The Ruse

(In which Sofia helps Ebby keep a seemingly impossible promise.)

"Does Soto still eat bread and cheese every day?" Sofia asked Ebby.

"Yes, he does." Ebby wondered what Sofia had in mind. George told her he loved fish guts, not dry old bread. She could not see how this would help her keep her promise to George.

"We should go see George and give him some, but not in the way he would expect," Sofia said smiling. Still not sure what Sofia was up to, Ebby hopped over to the table under the olive tree and brought some bread crusts and dried cheese to Sofia. "Do you mind if we fly there? It'll be much quicker." Ebby nodded and wiggled her tail enthusiastically. She never expected to fly with a dragon. Sofia grasped Ebby carefully in her clawed hand and flapped her wings. They rose off the ground and flew towards Roveen.

Ebby surveyed the ground far below her as they flew over the land. The enormous trees in Soto's farm reminded her of blades of grass, and the boulders along the shore looked like pebbles. Sofia shared her plan with Ebby on the way. When they arrived near the docks they saw George C. Gull sitting alone on his favorite wooden post having a detailed one-sided conversation with himself. "He's probably talking about food," Ebby guessed out loud. Sofia chuckled.

Sofia landed quietly on the dock behind George so he would not see them and set Ebby down. Ebby scampered close to George and said, "Oh my goodness! Look! There is a hungry purple sea dragon over there. I have some tasty food to give the hungry dragon." George stopped chattering. He followed Ebby's gaze to the enormous purple dragon standing on the dock. He had never seen a dragon before and did not know what kind of food they ate. It did not matter to him though because he knew instantly he wanted whatever Ebby had more than anything else in his entire life.

After making sure she had George's attention, Ebby approached Sofia carefully, holding the bread and cheese in front of her so George could not see what it was. When she got close, she dropped the food scraps between Sofia's feet saying loudly, "Here, hungry dragon. You are so big! You must be starving! I brought some tasty food for you to eat."

Sofia licked her lips and responded equally as loud. "Oh thank you, little bunny! I am so hungry. This food is the tastiest treat I have ever seen, and it's mine to eat all by myself! I cannot wait to..." Before Sofia could finish her sentence, George swooped over, grabbed the bread and cheese, and flew back to his perch. He swallowed the food whole before landing. Although he did not taste it, he knew nothing in the world had ever been more delicious.

Ebby approached George on his perch and pretended to be upset he had stolen the food from Sofia. "I hope you enjoyed that food, George!" she said as angrily as she could, considering she did not know how to be angry. "It was supposed to be eaten by that hungry dragon over there." Ebby pointed at Sofia.

George twittered with joy. "That was the best food I have ever eaten! I have stolen a fish from a fisherman and fish guts from my best friends, but nothing could possibly be as tasty as food stolen from a hungry dragon! This is the best day of my life!" He excused himself and flew away to join some gulls gathered around a little girl eating a pastry to tell them about the delicious meal he just ate.

Ebby and Sofia watched as George stood in the center of his gull friends bragging to them about what just happened. He pointed at Sofia to prove he was not lying. Sofia did her best to act miserable and disappointed that George had stolen her food. The other gulls chattered loudly and patted George on his back with their wings. As more gulls arrived to see what the commotion was about, stories were shrieked from gull to gull about George's bravery for stealing the tastiest morsels ever eaten by a gull right out from under a hungry dragon's nose.

Ebby's heart melted to see George at the center of attention surrounded by his friends. The plan worked perfectly and Sofia helped Ebby keep her promise to George. Just like Ebby, Sofia knew making others happy was the best feeling in the world.

CHAPTER SIXTEEN

Frisky's Big Decision

(In which Frisky listens to her heart.)

Not wanting to create more of a scene on the dock, Sofia scooped Ebby up and flew back to Soto's house. Soto and Frisky arrived a short time later. The four of them laughed about making George think he was stealing food from a hungry dragon. There was no doubt George had the absolutely best day of his life.

Then Frisky told Ebby her big news. "I am going to stay in Roveen with Ivan LeKar and become a writer. He has written many books about the history of the Land of Stones. He knows all about the ancient people who built Roveen and Slune hundreds, if not thousands, of years ago. I want to learn how to read and write so I can write my own stories. Ivan hasn't worked with a baby fox before. He thinks I'll be the first fox writer in the Land of Stones! He offered to let me stay with him and become his student."

Ebby knew she would miss her sweet friend, but Frisky was listening to her heart. Ebby congratulated Frisky and they talked about how much fun it would be for Frisky to write about their adventures.

After they had discussed Frisky's decision, Ebby said to Sofia, "We should travel the world together and see everything there is to see and do everything there is to do!"

"I was about to say the same thing!" Sofia replied enthusiastically. "After all, what else could an Elusive Baby Bunny and a magical purple sea dragon do?"

CHAPTER SEVENTEEN

The Creation of Magical Moments

*(In which the friends explore the area around
Roveen and Ebby ponders life's experiences.)*

The four friends spent the next several days exploring the area around Roveen as they prepared for their future adventures. They stayed at Soto's farm because they did not want to cause a commotion by having a dragon around.

Soto took them deep into the surrounding forest to see ancient ruins hidden by old trees and dense brush. He showed them places in the forest where old towns and fortresses used to stand. They found stone columns that once supported great roofs lying on

the ground next to broken marble statues. Soto was certain no one else had seen them in hundreds of years. The ruins were all that were left.

Over hundreds of years trees and vines grew between the cracks in the stone walls as if the forest was trying to reclaim the land. The tree roots and vines simultaneously tore the rock walls apart and held them together.

The ruins reminded Frisky of her own home. "I wonder what happened to the people who use to live where I grew up. I've never wondered about that before."

"Perhaps Ivan will help you research and write about it," Soto suggested.

Ebby described the broken statue she saw in the river on her way to Slune. Soto replied, "There are ancient treasures all over the Land of Stones. Some have been discovered but there are many more waiting to be found. Perhaps they'll be discovered by an Elusive Baby Bunny." The idea of finding ancient treasures captivated Ebby's imagination.

"I have seen amazing things deep under the Big Sea, like the old shipwreck I discovered a few days ago not far from one of the Stone Islands. I was going to investigate it further when I heard Soto calling me," Sofia said.

Sofia and Soto took the opportunity they had together to teach Ebby and Frisky how to swim. They thought it was necessary after Ebby described how they waded into the Big Sea to get to Roveen. It came naturally to both of them even though bunnies and foxes usually avoided water.

Frisky asked Sofia and Soto lots of questions about their lives. Ivan LeKar had told her it was important to ask the right questions and to listen carefully to the answers in order to become a good writer. This gave Frisky an excellent opportunity to hone her skills.

Ebby listened to Sofia answer Frisky's questions. It was enchanting to hear Sofia describe her adventures, but Ebby wanted to experience everything herself. She tried to imagine the sights, smells, and sounds of the far-off places Sofia had been, but Ebby knew her imagination was limited by her own personal experiences. How could she describe a carrot to her mother that would be as good as actually eating one? The sight of a carrot was not enough to remind Napoleon of his youth, but one taste of the tiny carrot pieces launched him into his memories as if he was reliving them. She wanted every moment to be that vivid.

Although Soto was not embarking on a new career or adventure himself, the enthusiasm surrounding him gave him a sense of fulfillment and joy. It made him feel young, and he knew it would give him plenty to think about after everyone left on their adventures. There was something about his friends' anticipation in starting new adventures that gave him an extra burst of creative energy he would later channel into his paintings.

The days they spent together were full of joy and wonder. They would always have these shared experiences. Memories of this time would make them smile years later. That was one of the lessons Ebby was learning about friendship. She made a point to savor each moment. She focused on how Frisky's eyes lit up with glee when Ebby said or did something funny or how Soto smiled and absentmindedly rubbed his beard when he showed them something new. She knew these were the things that would keep them close to her heart when they were far apart. All she would have to do is close her eyes and remember back to these days playing in the woods and sea around Roveen.

CHAPTER EIGHTEEN

Planning for the Future

(In which the adventures of Ebby and Sofia are discussed.)

During the day the four friends explored the forests and ancient ruins. At night Ebby and Sofia stared at the stars and discussed where they should go next. The world was vast, and there were so many places to visit. Sofia wanted to take Ebby to the shipwreck she discovered. She was certain Ebby would enjoy exploring the depths of the sea. Swimming underwater was easy for Sofia. She could swim for hours without coming up for air. Ebby had never been underwater and it was something no other dragon and Elusive Baby Bunny had done together. The biggest issue was figuring out how to safely take a baby bunny underwater with her. Ebby had learned how to swim, but she would not be able to hold her breath long enough to reach the shipwreck.

Sofia needed something she could transport Ebby in that would allow her to breathe underwater while protecting her from the enormous pressure at the bottom of the sea. She found the solution while staring at the moon. The shape of the partially full moon made her think of the egg she was born in. The eggshell protected her from the outside world while she was forming into a baby dragon and allowed her to breathe until she was ready to come out.

A dragon eggshell was made of diamond crystals. This made it so strong it would not break under the pressure of the sea. The egg was clear so Ebby would be able to see through it. It was large enough for a baby bunny to have plenty of room and have enough air to breathe. Most importantly she knew where to find one. For generations Sofia's family kept all their eggshells in a cave deep under the ocean in the Land of Dragons. She would fly to the cave and retrieve it.

Sofia left the next morning. She planned to visit her family while she was there and return the following day. She could not wait to tell her grandfather she had met an Elusive Baby Bunny.

Meanwhile, Soto left to paint in his Roveen studio. He had some ideas about painting fantastical landscapes with ruins and magical creatures, drawing on the time he had spent in the forest with Ebby, Sofia, and Frisky.

This gave Ebby and Frisky one more day together before they followed their different paths. They chased butterflies, went swimming, and walked around in the forest. They had come a long way together since meeting at Frisky's Rocks. Frisky remembered gazing across the Big Sea at Roveen from the window ledge of the ruins. She never thought she would travel this far let alone study to be a writer. She had Ebby to thank for this. She wanted to tell the world about Sofia's adventures, Ebby's travels, and the ancient history of the Land of Stones. She dreamed of getting to be the one who taught Rip about giraffes, elephants, and hippopotamuses. She imagined the expressions he would make the first time he heard about them.

Ebby thought Frisky's idea was brilliant. Anyone who was not able to travel the world and experience it on their own could still learn about them. Frisky's books would bring the adventures to everyone.

As for Ebby, she woke up every morning wondering what new things would happen to her and went to sleep each night dreaming about what she had done. This constantly drove her forward. She knew she would always be saying goodbye to old friends, but she would also always be saying hello to new ones. That was at the heart of what made her an Elusive Baby Bunny.

CHAPTER NINETEEN

The Dragon Egg

(In which Ebby discovers the vastness and smallness of the world.)

As promised, Sofia returned from the Land of Dragons the next day. She carried her dragon eggshell in a purple bag made of strong silk. Ebby, Frisky, and Soto gathered around her as she pulled the eggshell out of the bag. They gasped in awe at its brilliance and shine. It was like nothing they had seen before. The surface of the shell was smooth and shaped like a chicken egg, but it was much bigger. It was clear like beautiful, flawless glass and it shimmered in the sunlight. The rays of the sun created an unusual glow that came from inside the shell itself.

The shell was made entirely of diamond crystals and was therefore virtually unbreakable. The only thing that could break a diamond dragon eggshell was the sweet trill of the baby dragon ready to come out of the egg. Sofia remembered that exact moment. A sweet vibrating sound came deep from her heart and caused the egg to break into two equal pieces. It came to her as if by magic, and she was never able to make that sound again.

Sofia removed the top piece of the shell with one hand

and put the bottom half of the shell on the ground. "Climb in, Ebby." Without a second thought Ebby jumped in. She had lots of space to move around. Sofia picked it up and placed the upper piece on top of the bottom piece, completely enclosing Ebby inside the shell. She spoke to Ebby to make sure she could still hear her and had plenty of air inside to breathe. Although Sofia could not hear Ebby speak inside the egg, Ebby nodded and smiled when she heard Sofia's voice. Ebby could see clearly, almost as if the shell was invisible. The diamond crystals made everything appear bigger.

Sofia removed the top of the shell and asked Ebby what she thought. "I feel your love and warmth surrounding me." Sofia was so moved a diamond tear dropped with a soft thud on the ground.

Sofia asked Soto if he had some beeswax. She explained she could use beeswax to seal the two halves together, making the shell waterproof for their underwater adventure. Soto left to get some beeswax from the beehive in his olive grove.

"We could swim to the shipwreck, but it's a long way to go underwater and I think you'll enjoy flying more." Ebby agreed.

Ebby jumped out of the egg and hugged Frisky. "You are the best friend anyone could ever want. I promise to come back and tell you all my adventures so you can write about them." She then told Soto, who had returned with the beeswax, "Thank you so much, Soto! You taught Frisky to listen to her heart, and I know she is going to become a great writer. I promise to come back and let you paint me." Finally, she turned her attention to Sofia. "We've got things to do and places to go! Let's start by going to the bottom of the sea!"

Ebby jumped into the eggshell. Soto applied some of the

beeswax around the edge of the bottom piece and placed the top of the shell into place. Sofia blew on the wax, heating it with her breath just enough to make it soft and pressed the two halves firmly together. Soto handed Sofia some extra beeswax to take with her if she needed it to reseal the egg later. Sofia put the beeswax in the silk pouch and tied it to one of her clawed hands. Sofia picked up the egg and started flapping her wings and flew into the sky.

"Goodbye, my friends," Sofia called down to them. Ebby waved goodbye. She watched as Soto and Frisky faded out of sight, followed by the farm, then Roveen. Soon all Ebby could see was the beautiful turquoise water of the Big Sea glistening below her. The small white tops of the waves moved in rhythm. The water was so clear Ebby saw to the bottom of the sea in all but the deepest spots. She saw mountains and deep valleys under the water. Large schools of fish swam through beds of seaweed.

Sofia flew over hundreds of islands known as the Stone Islands scattered throughout the Big Sea. Some of the islands were uninhabited and covered with thick forests. Other islands had fields of grapes and olive trees with small farms like Soto's. Others were completely bare, consisting only of rocks and stones beaten by the waves. The Big Sea stretched as far as Ebby could see.

At midday, Sofia located an island covered with grass and flowers on one end and a thick forest on the other. Rocky cliffs jutted a hundred feet out of the water and circled the entire island. Waves crashed against the cliffs. No one other than a flying dragon could safely land on this island.

With a soft upward swish of her wings Sofia landed in the

field of flowers. She made sure the island was safe for Ebby before opening the egg. "How did you enjoy the flight?"

Ebby was speechless at first. It felt strange to be on the ground again at baby bunny height. She never imagined she would be able to view the world as she had just done. Only a few weeks earlier the highest she had been was standing on Chip's log in Fluffle Valley peeking over the top of grass and flowers for the first time. Now she was flying through the air with a purple sea dragon. "I felt like I was the biggest and the smallest creature in the world at the same time. I could see everything at once, but it made me see how small I am." Sofia smiled. She remembered how she felt the first time she flew above the sea in the Land of Dragons.

"Flying always makes me hungry. I saw a Dragon Tree on the other side of the island. Why don't you eat something here," Sofia suggested, "and I'll get a bite to eat as well. I'll be back soon and then we can explore the shipwreck."

While Sofia flew off to the forested area of the island to get something to eat, Ebby ate her fill of delicious orange and pink flowers. It had been an eventful day. The sun warmed her back as she ate, and before she knew it she had fallen asleep. Sofia returned a short time later to find Ebby curled up in a little ball. The rush of wind from Sofia's wings stirred the fur on Ebby's back and quietly woke her from her nap. She was not sure how long she had been asleep, but she felt rested and ready to dive down into the sea.

Ebby jumped back into the bottom half of the eggshell. Sofia placed the other half on top and blew on the beeswax until it was soft. She then pressed the two halves together tightly, forming a tight seal to protect Ebby from water leaking into the egg. When Sofia was certain the egg was properly sealed, she cradled it in her claws and flew to the end of the island. She landed on a cliff overlooking the sea. Waves crashed into the rocks far below them.

Sofia pointed to a spot in the sea off in the distance. "That's where I saw the shipwreck. We're going there next."

The Land of Stones

PART TWO

The Adventures of Ebby and Sofia

CHAPTER TWENTY

Under the Sea

*(In which Sofia and Ebby explore the
underwater world and find treasure.)*

Standing on the cliffs high above the Big Sea, Sofia brought the egg close to her face so Ebby could hear her. "We won't be able to talk while underwater," Sofia told Ebby. "Tap on the shell if you need to communicate with me." Ebby nodded that she understood.

The sea beyond the cliffs was calm as Sofia flew over. The water was so clear Ebby felt she could reach out and touch the sea floor. Sofia dove into the water. The sound of the wind encircling the shell stopped at once as they entered the water with a large splash. It became strangely quiet inside the eggshell. At first all Ebby could see were millions of tiny bubbles created by the splash of them entering the water. As Sofia swam down, the water cleared. Ebby heard the faint sound of Sofia's wings and feet moving the water as she swam. Deeper and deeper they went.

Ebby looked around in amazement. The light from the sun penetrated the surface of the water creating a strange golden glow. Sunrays lit up the seafloor in bright yellow spots. The undersea world shimmered. The diamond crystal eggshell slightly distorted her view. Ebby saw a large, dark, blurry object in the distance coming straight towards them. She watched as the size and shape of the object changed constantly. When the object was nearly upon them, Ebby realized it was not a single sea creature but a large school of small fish swimming tightly together.

As soon as the fish caught sight of Sofia, they parted into two groups turning sharply to avoid running into her. The fish surrounded Sofia and Ebby. Some of the fish came within inches of Ebby's wide eyes. They were brilliantly colored, some had spots, others had stripes, some even had long tails and flowing fins. Ebby had never seen anything so colorful. They vanished as quickly as they arrived.

Larger fish swam alone or in smaller groups. The bigger fish were not as colorful as the smaller ones. They did not mind a purple sea dragon in their midst even though Sofia was much bigger than them. They darted swiftly to safety when Sofia got too close but ignored her the rest of the time. Sofia enjoyed that her presence did not upset anyone underwater like it often did on land.

Once they reached the bottom of the sea, Ebby saw dark jagged rocks covered with colorful underwater plants. The plants swayed back and forth with the current. They reminded Ebby of flowers being blown by the wind. Different types of fish swam in between the sea plants. Their petals opened and closed as fish swam close to them.

Sofia swam until she reached a wide opening in the sea floor covered by sand and coral reefs. Ebby saw objects similar to the old stone statues in the forest near Roveen. Although they were broken and partially covered with sea creatures and sand, Ebby could tell one was a statue of a woman. A greenish blue statue rested on the seabed mostly covered by sand. The movement of the water caused by Sofia's wings swept the sand away exposing the statue of a man.

Just beyond the statues they approached a large wooden structure. They had reached the shipwreck. The ship was much larger than the fishing boats tied to the dock in Roveen. The ship was broken into several pieces and scattered over a wide area. Sand and coral covered many sections of the ship. Jagged wooden planks from the ship's frame jutted out of the seabed.

As Sofia swam around the shipwreck, the front of the ship lying on its side came into view. Hundreds of fish swam in and out of a large hole in the hull. Ebby guessed the hole was caused when the ship sank. Large ceramic pots and big boxes made of wood lay in shambles on either side of the ship's ruins. One of the boxes had broken open. Gold pieces, jewelry, and small golden statues rested inside the box and were scattered in the sand. Ebby thought she saw a shape that reminded her of Frisky. She tapped on the eggshell so Sofia could hear her and pointed at the box. Sofia nodded and swam closer to the broken box. She knocked the lid off completely with a gentle wave of her tail so they could see what was inside. The lid floated to the sand and came to a rest.

Lying on top of the gold pieces in the box was a golden scepter with a fox head. It looked just like Frisky! Sofia picked it up and put it in the purple silk bag where she had carried her eggshell. Sofia swam around the shipwreck poking her head inside the holes and crevices too small for her to swim through. She held the egg up so Ebby could see too. They found bright white pillars made of marble lying in pieces deep inside the ship. They were like the broken columns Soto showed them in the ruins around Roveen. There was no trace of the people who had sailed on this ship, but they could have been the same people who built the villages and towns in the Land of Stones.

After exploring the shipwreck a bit longer, Sofia started swimming back to the island so Ebby would not run out of air. She went through deep narrow canyons and large kelp forests. They saw dolphins, whales, octopuses, and other unusual sea creatures no bunny saw before. Soon, Ebby heard the sound of distant waves crashing against the rocks as they neared the island. The sun got brighter and brighter as Sofia swam towards the surface. They burst out of the water, with Sofia flying straight up above the cliffs. She landed softly then opened the egg to let Ebby out.

"How did you enjoy our first adventure together?" Sofia asked Ebby.

Ebby wriggled her little white bunny tail and motioned for Sofia to lower her head. Sofia bent down so her face almost touched Ebby's. Ebby jumped up on her back legs and gave Sofia a big kiss on her nose. "That was the most wondrous experience

I could possibly imagine! I had no idea there was so much life in the sea! I didn't know fish could be so beautiful and colorful or that plants grew under the water. It was so different from anything I've seen before."

"I'm so happy you enjoyed it!" Sofia replied joyfully. She was touched by Ebby's reaction. "Although I don't live in the Big Sea, it's similar to where I used to play with my friends in the Land of Dragons. Many of the things you thought were plants were actually living animals that grow on rocks. They don't have arms or legs but they still have mouths and brains. They need food and sunlight to grow. Even the kelp in the underwater canyon needs sunlight to survive."

Ebby asked Sofia about the shipwreck. "What do you think happened to the people who sailed on that ship and what will happen to the beautiful things we saw down there?"

"I don't know what happened to the people on the ship. Ships carrying valuable statues and gold often traveled with other ships, so I'm certain the people were saved. By the look of all the sea life growing on the ruins, I think it sank a long time ago. The statues and golden items will likely remain on the sea floor for the rest of time until the sand and shells completely cover them up—or until someone like us finds them." Sofia winked and smiled at Ebby. She pulled the golden scepter out of the silk bag. It sparkled brilliantly in the sun as if it had just been made. "I think this will make a lovely present for Frisky, don't you?" Ebby nodded. It would make a spectacular gift.

CHAPTER TWENTY-ONE

The Wall and the Cliffs

(In which Ebby and Sofia discover a village with no visitors.)

That night Ebby and Sofia sat on a cliff high above the Big Sea and watched the sun set. They discussed where they should go next. Sofia told Ebby about a village she flew over on an island called Zidani. The village was built on the side of a cliff far above the water. She could not find anyone who had been to Zidani even though it was in the middle of the Big Sea. "This would be fun for our next adventure."

The next morning Sofia put her dragon eggshell and Frisky's present into the silk bag. She flew to the forest on the far side of the island and tied the bag to the highest limb of a Dragon Tree where she knew it would be safe. After eating some tasty Dragon Fruit, she returned just as Ebby was finishing her breakfast. Ebby climbed into Sofia's clawed hand, and they flew towards Zidani Island.

This time Ebby was not inside Sofia's egg. She felt the wind blowing through her fur and whiskers as they flew high above the sea. She loved how the wind tickled her eyelashes. She thought of Napoleon Ponyparte and how he loved the sound of the wind singing in his ears when he galloped through the fields as a frisky colt.

She stared down at the clear blue water below her. She now knew the sea was full of living creatures. It was not just a big empty expanse of water like she assumed when she saw it for the first time. It was a home for all the underwater creatures she saw. Next time she was underwater she would definitely take some yummy yellow flowers and thank the fish for letting her visit their home.

This new perspective made Ebby wonder what a fish would think if one visited her fluffle. She was certain a fish would find her home as strange and unexpected as it had been for her to visit the sea.

Sofia flew south until she spotted Zidani Island. She pointed to a village built along the edge of cliffs high above the Big Sea. The houses were so close to one another there was no room between them. The ones closest to the edge of the cliff were only one story high. The houses behind the first row were two stories high. The second story still had a view of the sea, but the lower level was completely blocked from sight. Each house farther back from the sea was one story higher than the row of houses in front of it. The houses farthest from the cliff were the tallest, but only the top floor could be seen. Some of the houses were so skinny they seemed to have been added later to fill a small opening between two larger homes.

The village was surrounded by a massive stone wall on three sides. Only the front of the village opened to the sea. The wall was taller than any of the houses inside the village. As a result, the only light hitting the houses was coming from the cliff side. The paths between the houses were even more narrow and crooked than the ones in Roveen. It was dark inside the village.

At first glance it appeared like the only way to get into the village was from the air (if you happened to be a dragon). As they got closer, however, Sofia saw a rope ladder hanging from the top of the cliff to a small sandy beach hundreds of feet below. Jagged cliffs and sharp rocks surrounded the beach. The only way to access the village was to climb up the ladder.

There was a man on the ladder carrying a large bag tied to his back. He wiped the sweat from his forehead and looked down at the beach to see how far he had gone. He sighed when he realized he still had a long way to go and continued climbing. Five men stood in line on the beach with large bags tied to their backs waiting their turn to climb the ladder. Meanwhile a sailor unloaded bags of fruits, vegetables, and fish on the sand for several more men.

Sofia's shadow briefly passed over the beach. The men panicked when Sofia temporarily blocked out the sun and saw her flying high above them. They yelled frantically at the man on the ladder to warn him about the dragon in the sky. Upon hearing the yells, the man on the ladder looked at where they were pointing. He saw Sofia flying high above him and panicked because he had no place to hide. He scrambled faster up the ladder and nearly lost his footing in the process. One of his shoes came off and fell to the beach, nearly hitting the men standing below him. The men on the beach did not have

anywhere to hide either. They stood frozen in place with their mouths open.

Sofia continued flying towards the village unaware of the panic she created far below her. She hoped to find a place to land, but the houses were too tightly huddled together. There were no parks or open spaces anywhere inside the wall. The dark narrow paths between the buildings were hardly wide enough for two people to pass, let alone provide enough space for a dragon to land. Sofia flew over the wall on the far side of the village. Several men stood on the wall carrying sticks. They were terrified when they saw Sofia flying overhead.

The land on the other side of the wall was bright and sunny. Fruit filled the trees and tall grass swayed in the wind. It was beautiful and reminded Ebby of her home. There were no houses, barns, or fenced fields; nor were there any horses, cows, or roosters. "Why doesn't anyone live here? There is so much space on this side of the wall."

"I don't know." Just as Sofia was about to turn back towards the village she saw something moving. "I think I see something. Let's see what it is."

Sofia flew closer and recognized the movement as the flickering of a donkey tail. The donkey slept in the shade of a lemon tree. Her dark fur blended into the shadow making her almost invisible. Sofia landed quietly near the donkey. She did not want to startle her from her nap, so she whispered to Ebby to wake her up and find out what she knew about the village. Ebby hopped over to the donkey, stood up on her hind legs, and said, "Excuse me. My name is Ebby. I am visiting your island with my friend, Sofia. Can you please help us?"

The donkey was in a deep sleep. Her tail twitched a bit

more. Ebby waited, but the donkey did not move. Ebby cleared her throat trying to get the donkey's attention. One of the donkey's ears moved in Ebby's direction while the other ear stayed still. Ebby cleared her throat again a little louder. This time the donkey lazily opened an eye. She lifted her head and focused on Sofia standing a little farther away from the baby bunny who was talking to her. The donkey shook her head, as if trying to wake up from a dream.

Ebby repeated, "Excuse me. My name is Ebby. I am visiting your island with my friend, Sofia. Can you please help us?"

The donkey sat up. "I'm Alotta Burrotta. Is that a dragon?" Ebby nodded her head. Alotta blinked her eyes several times as if they were playing tricks on her. "How did you get here? I've lived here for years and no one has been on this side of the wall."

"We flew," Ebby said. She pointed to Sofia.

Sofia's wings, body, and tail sparkled in the sunlight. Sofia's eyes instantly assured Alotta she had nothing to fear. She got up and trotted to Sofia. Ebby hopped past Alotta to sit between Sofia's front legs. "How can I help you?"

"Can you tell us why everyone lives on the other side of the wall in that village when there is so much space on this side?" Sofia asked. "I couldn't find a place to land. There were people getting food from a boat and carrying it up the side of the cliff. Why don't they just get it from this side of the wall? You have oranges, lemons, and pomegranates. And why is the wall so high? How is anyone supposed to get inside?"

Alotta sighed. She did not know what to say about the people behind the wall because she did not understand it herself. "I came to Zidani Island several years ago with my friend Paulo. 'Zidani' means 'wall' in the Land of Stones and the island is called Zidani because of that enormous wall. The village itself does not have a name even though it has been there for hundreds of years. The villagers never leave the village. Never. No outsider has ever been allowed inside the village either."

Sofia and Ebby were confused. Ebby asked, "You mean you have never been inside the village?" Alotta shook her head. "And no one in the village has ever been out here?"

"No. You are the first visitors I've had. It's nice to have someone to talk to. It gets pretty lonely, even if I can eat and sleep whenever I want."

"What are you doing here all by yourself? How did you get

here?" Ebby asked.

"That's a long story," Alotta replied. "Do you have time to hear it all?"

"Of course! That's why we came here."

"I was hoping you would say that! This is the most excitement I've had in years!" Alotta shook her head like she was trying to knock the cobwebs out of her ears and flicked her tail excitedly.

"The villagers make the most beautiful gold jewelry in the Land of Stones. It's extremely valuable and difficult to get. Even a small ring or necklace is worth a fortune. They don't sell the jewelry. The only way to get some is to trade it for food or other items the villagers need. It's a closely guarded secret.

"My friend Paulo learned about it from an old sailor who used to trade food and clothing for their gold jewelry. The villagers allowed a few sailors to land on the beach below the village. After they were certain the sailor was trustworthy, they would lower their ladder and climb down to the beach to see what they had to exchange. Each time they would take a little bit of jewelry with them to trade with the sailors. That is what you saw happening on the beach.

"Paulo didn't want to wait years to accumulate a little bit of their jewelry. He wanted to buy a lot of their jewelry at once and sell it back home. He thought he could become rich overnight and hoped to be the first person the villagers would allow into the village. He asked me to come with him so I could help him carry the jewelry. I have a strong back and sturdy legs. I carried rocks and bricks all day in our town. I didn't care about the jewelry, but sailing to this island sounded relaxing, so I joined him.

"But it wasn't a relaxing trip. The entire island is surrounded by cliffs and jagged rocks. It's easy to sail to the beach, but no one is allowed to land unless they have something to trade. The villagers don't let anyone climb their ladder. They pull it up each night so no one can enter the village.

"We landed on the beach first, but since the villagers didn't know Paulo, and we didn't have anything to trade, they didn't come down. We left the beach and sailed around the island to see if there was some other way to get in. There's one other place on the opposite side of the island where you can come ashore. The tide is only high enough a couple of times a year for a small boat to land without getting smashed to pieces on the rocks. That's exactly where Paulo said we should go.

"It was difficult to sail through the rocks and rolling waves. I'm a donkey, not a sailor. I didn't like it at all. After a few hours of getting tossed around in the sea I started wishing I was back home carrying bricks and rocks all day. Once we made it to the shore, it took several more days to walk here. We didn't see any other people or animals on the island, just some crazy birds that fought over whatever they found to eat." Ebby and Sofia laughed. They knew Alotta was talking about gulls.

"When we finally reached the wall, we walked its entire length. There were no doors or gates anywhere. The wall ended at the edge of the cliffs and we couldn't get around it. Paulo called out to the guards on top of the wall and asked if we could come inside. They told us strangers weren't allowed inside the village.

"We went to a different part of the wall, and Paulo asked the guards there to let him in, hoping to get a different answer. They also refused. They said they'd build the wall higher if we didn't leave them alone. Paulo wanted to wait a little longer to see if they'd change their minds. We camped below the wall. After a few days, the guards started adding large stones to the top of the wall, making it even higher. Paulo reluctantly concluded he would never be allowed in the village and needed to go home.

"I walked back to the boat with him but told him I wanted to stay here. I didn't enjoy the boat ride and didn't want to sail again. The island is beautiful on this side of the wall, and the air smells like honey. I can eat as much as I want and I don't have to carry heavy loads of bricks and stones all day. I can sleep whenever and wherever I want. Plus, I never have to worry about danger because I'm the only one living on this side of the wall. But it is lonely here. I wish I had someone to talk to and do things with."

Ebby and Sofia could not imagine why the entire village kept itself locked away from the rest of the island. Zidani Island was large enough for each family to have a big piece of land. It was clearly safe enough since Alotta was the only one who lived on this side of the wall. It did not make sense why the villagers stayed on the other side of the wall.

"Are you thinking what I'm thinking?" Sofia asked Ebby with a twinkle in her eye.

"Absolutely! Let's find out what's going on."

CHAPTER TWENTY-TWO

The Village on the Cliff

(In which Ebby and Sofia teach the Villagers of Zidani
that love and kindness are stronger than fear.)

D ragons are phenomenal. For one thing dragons can fly. Although the villagers built a wall impossible to climb, it would never be tall enough to keep a dragon out. The only tricky part was finding a place to land.

Sofia and Ebby circled high above the village hunting for a roof big enough to land on and wide enough for Sofia to spread her wings when she took off. There was only one place that met her requirements: the tallest house in the village. It was close to the wall and had a large flat roof where she could land. Since it was taller than the buildings around it, she

would be able to flap her wings without knocking into them.

Sofia landed silently on the roof. They could see the entire village from this spot. Colorful red tiles covered the jumbled roofs and the sea shimmered in the distance. The only thing behind them was the big ugly grey wall. It was much taller than the building they were standing on. It cast a grim shadow everywhere.

Sofia set Ebby down so she could explore the roof without making noise. Over the side of the building, Ebby saw a balcony that ran the length of the top story. Several people stood on the balcony dressed in plain clothing. A few of the women wore beautiful gold necklaces, bracelets, earrings, and rings. Some men wore gold chains around their necks. A few of the elderly villagers held canes covered with gold and set with precious jewels. The jewelry sparkled brilliantly in the sun. Ebby noted the jewelry was the only thing bright and cheery in this village. Everything else was grey and drab, including the people. The villagers were discussing something serious. Some cried. Others had bright red faces and were visibly upset. Ebby could hear them from her perch on the roof.

"What should we do?" a beautiful young woman cried out. "The dragon will surely rain fire and destruction upon us! Our village will be ruined! What's left of our beautiful jewelry will be stolen! What will happen to us then when we can no longer afford to buy food?"

Another yelled, "We need to build the wall higher. If we build it high enough, surely the dragon can't get over it and we will be safe."

A tall man with a black hat said, "The dragon can fly over any wall we build. We need to build a roof, which will cover the entire village. Only by protecting us from the sky will we ever be safe!"

A different man replied, "It would take us years to build a roof to cover the whole village. Where would we get the materials to build it? As it is, it takes us several days to bring food up the ladder to feed our families."

A new voice bellowed, "We should build a roof! The wall is not enough. We can tear down some of the houses and use the rocks and wooden beams to build it."

An old man who had not spoken before asked meekly, "But whose houses will we tear down to build the roof? We already have too many people living in the houses as it is. If we tear down some of the houses, where will those people live?"

To which the tall man said, "We can add more stories to our other houses, and the people can live there."

"But what about my view?" another villager replied. "How will I see the sky and the sea if you build a taller house in front of me? I already can't see anything from my window unless I stand on a chair."

The tall man in the black hat clapped his hands loudly and asked for silence. "I am the mayor of this village. I am therefore the wisest. It will not matter whether we can see the sky or the sea if our village is destroyed by this mighty dragon. No one will be able to see the sky and the sea if we build a roof over the entire village! We will all suffer, but we will all be safe together." Several men started pointing to houses they could tear down to make the roof.

Ebby was stunned. They had not even met Sofia and were already so afraid of her they were willing to block out the sky and tear down their own homes. Diamond tears of sadness dropped from Sofia's eyes onto the roof. It sounded like big drops of rain falling. Ebby could not stay silent any longer.

Ebby stood up on the edge of the roof and addressed the crowd on the balcony below her. "Sofia is my friend, and she would never hurt you or anyone else. She is the most wonderful, kind, beautiful, and exceptional dragon you will ever meet." Sofia smiled weakly. She tried to stop crying but was sad she frightened people who did not know her. Small diamond tears dropped steadily on the roof.

The group of villagers were shocked. They could not see Sofia because she was standing away from the edge of the roof. They only saw a baby bunny on the tallest building of a village no stranger had visited for hundreds of years.

"What are you doing on my roof?" the mayor demanded. "Who are you? Where did you come from? How did you get around our wall? How do you know this horrible dragon doesn't want to destroy our village and steal our valuable jewelry?"

Ebby stood taller and straighter than she had ever stood. "I am Ebby. I'm an Elusive Baby Bunny. I was born in Fluffle Valley in the Land of Stones. I left my home because I wanted to see everything there is to see and do everything there is to do. I traveled here with my friend Sofia. She's from the Land of Dragons. We didn't come here to destroy your village or take anything from you. We don't want you to tear down your houses. We don't want you to block out the sky so you'll never be able to see the sun and the stars. We only came to visit you and make friends."

The mayor, whose name was Darko, replied doubtfully, "I have never heard of an Elusive Baby Bunny, but we have heard stories about dragons who breathe fire and destroy all they see. How do we know you did not come to destroy us?"

Ebby thought about it for a second. It was true the villagers did not know anything about her or Sofia. She heard the fear in their voices and knew it was real. They did not know she and Sofia were only capable of love, kindness, and friendship. She glanced back at the wall surrounding the village. It successfully kept everyone out until today, but it also kept the villagers trapped inside.

Darko repeated his question. "How do we know you did not come to destroy us?"

As Ebby struggled for the best words to say, Sofia moved to the edge of the roof so the villagers could see her. They gasped in terror at the sight of the large purple dragon on the roof. They clutched their golden necklaces and tried to hide them from her. Slowly, however, as they looked into Sofia's beautiful eyes, their expressions relaxed a bit. They lowered their hands. Ebby remembered exactly how she felt when she saw Sofia coming out of the water in response to Soto's bell. Sofia's eyes were the colors of the bluest sky and the most vibrant sunset all at once. There was nothing frightening about them.

Then Sofia spoke with the voice that always made Ebby think of flowers and happiness. "I understand you're afraid because you don't know me. But you shouldn't be afraid of everything you don't know. Sometimes the best possible things come from places we least expect. We've come here to be your friends, not to destroy your village. Please give us a chance to prove you don't have to be afraid of us."

Darko was comforted by the sound of Sofia's soothing voice. He was also relieved that she had not already destroyed his village, but he was still worried. "How do we know what to be afraid of? We've been taught that everything outside our village is bad."

Sofia replied, "The more you learn about the world, the less afraid of it you will become. And the more love and kindness there is, the less there is to fear. When two strangers meet and become friends, their friendship makes them *both* stronger and happier. They can help and teach each other new things. If two strangers meet and are afraid of each other, they stay strangers. Their fear makes them *both* weaker, sadder, and alone.

"Learning new things and making new friends is the best way to overcome your fear. Ebby is my friend. She is a tiny baby bunny. I am a dragon. We're different, and yet we are the best of friends. Let us get to know one another. If you're still afraid of us after we've spent some time together, we'll leave you alone forever."

The beautiful young woman who had feared Sofia would destroy the village and steal their jewelry responded loudly so everyone could hear, "Hello, Ebby and Sofia. I'm Manuela. I think we should give you a chance to be our friends before we tear down our houses and block out the sky. I'm tired of being afraid all the time. I'd like to listen to what you have to say." The rest of the villagers mumbled their agreement.

Sofia and Ebby took turns telling the villagers about their lives. Sofia told them some of her grand adventures and what she had seen on the other side of the world. Next Ebby revealed what it was like for her to see the world first from the top of a log, then from the back of a horse, then a mountain, then flying through the sky with Sofia. Each time she got a new view of the world she wanted to see more of it. She also told them of the friends she met along the way and how they had helped each other.

Together, Ebby and Sofia told the villagers about diving to the bottom of the sea, the beautiful and strange underwater creatures they saw, and finding the shipwreck. Lastly, they told them about meeting Alotta Burrotta and the lush unspoiled land on the other side of their wall.

The villagers were amazed. None of them had ever been outside their village except to climb down the ladder to get food and clothing from passing boats. Only the guards knew what was on the other side of the wall, and they were not allowed to speak about it. No one ever swam in the sea or ran through a field of grass and flowers. They had never seen a horse, a fox, a cow, a donkey, or a rooster. They had never heard of giraffes, hippopotamuses, or elephants. Everything Sofia and Ebby told them was new.

After Ebby and Sofia told them about their lives and experiences, it was Darko's turn to share the history of the village and its people.

CHAPTER TWENTY-THREE

The History from the Beginners to the Tallers

(In which Mayor Darko gives the history of his people.)

Darko was not only the mayor, he explained to Ebby and Sofia, he was also the village's official historian. He wrote down all important events and kept them in the Book of Pages, a book started hundreds of years earlier by the first people to settle the village. He was the only one in the village who was allowed to see the Book of Pages. Most villagers did not know the full history of their people and were hearing it for the first time. This surprised Ebby. "Why doesn't everyone know your history?"

"Our elders concluded long ago that it was better if we didn't know everything about our past. I'm not exactly sure why. Maybe they were afraid someone might try to leave the island and get lost again." He cleared his throat and began.

"Our history begins hundreds of years ago when our ancestors crossed the Big Sea in two large ships from a land far away. We don't know where they came from because it wasn't written in the Book of Pages. They were in search of a place to begin a new life with their families. The two ships carried a vast treasure of gold, stone carvings, and other valuables. The ships were caught in a fierce storm, and one of the ships sank after it crashed against rocks.

"All the people on the sinking ship were saved and brought aboard the remaining ship. Some of the gold was also saved, but much of the treasure sank. The surviving ship was barely big enough to

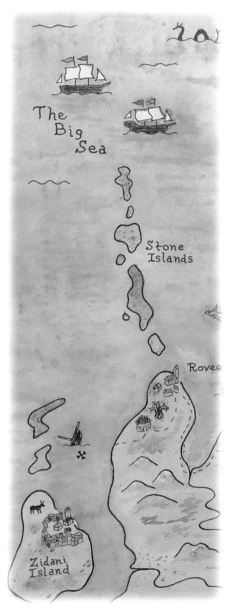

carry everyone, and they knew it would not get far. They spent several treacherous days at sea before they found this island. It was too dangerous for everyone to continue the journey on the surviving ship, so they left the people from the sunken ship on the beach below with their remaining treasure.

"No one lived on the island when they arrived, which is why the first people became known as the Beginners. The people aboard the other ship promised to return and take the Beginners to the new land they had hoped to discover together. They never returned, and so they became known as the Leavers.

"Several weeks after being left on the beach, the strongest Beginners climbed the cliff and discovered the land above. They made a ladder out of rope and lowered it down to the Beginners on the beach. Eventually everyone climbed to the top. Every day the Beginners took turns watching for the Leavers to return with a rescue ship, but the Leavers did not come.

"Eventually, the Beginners started building houses to keep themselves safe and warm while they waited for the Leavers to return. Some Beginners built houses near the edge of the cliff to keep watch for the Leavers' ship. A few Beginners built their homes away from the cliff in the middle of the island. They grew fruits and vegetables to feed the village. Each family was given an equal amount of the remaining gold treasure. They started making beautiful jewelry to pass the time.

"Many more years passed. By this time, all Beginners had built homes for their families, but they still waited for the day the Leavers would return to rescue them. The Beginners never named their village because they always expected the Leavers to return. One day, a small boat passed by the beach below carrying food and clothing from far away. Some Beginners climbed down the ladder and called to the passing boat. The sailors were surprised because they did not know anyone lived on the island. They landed on the beach and offered to trade for the gold jewelry the Beginners wore. The sailors did not have enough room on their boat to take any of the Beginners with them but promised to return.

"Several more months passed before the boat came to the island again. The sailors brought more food and again offered to exchange it for some of the Beginners' gold jewelry. Yet again they did not have room on their boat to take anyone with them, but once more promised to return. This happened several times over the following years. Each time food and other goods were exchanged for some of the gold jewelry made by the Beginners. Each time the sailors claimed they would return with a bigger boat to take the people home.

"Eventually the Beginners concluded the sailors were never going to rescue them, just as the Leavers had never returned. Some Beginners began to worry the sailors intended to come back at night while the Beginners slept and steal the rest of their treasure. Soon, the Beginners believed all sailors were bad people. Although they needed the food the sailors brought, they did not want the sailors to be able to come into the village and steal from them. They started to raise the rope ladder every night to keep the sailors out and moved their homes closer together for protection against the sailors. The Beginners who built their homes in the middle of the island tore them down and rebuilt them closer to the houses near the cliffs.

"Every family wanted a view of the sea in case the Leavers' ship passed by to rescue them. As a result, the entire village was built along the cliffs. Each house was promised at least one window looking over the sea. At this time the Beginners were still able to freely travel all over the island. They could tend to their gardens, and the children played in the fields. Some married and had children, and the number of people in the village continued to grow.

"One day a young boy asked why they raised the rope ladder every night when someone could just walk into the village from the other side of the island. No one had ever landed on the other side of the island because ragged rocks and waves made it very hazardous, but the Beginners started to build a wall around the village to make sure it was protected from all sides. At first the wall was small with a gate. To be safe, they moved their gardens inside the wall so the sailors couldn't steal their fruits and vegetables. The children were no longer allowed to play outside the wall, and the gate was locked each night."

The villagers on the balcony listening to Darko explain their history were shocked to hear that prior generations moved freely on the island and had grown their own fruits and vegetables on the other side of the wall. They shook their heads in disbelief.

Darko pressed on. "Years passed, and the villagers built more houses to support the growing population. The Beginners became more dependent on the sailors because they didn't have enough space to grow their own food inside the wall. The gold treasure shrank bit by bit each time the Beginners traded it. Each new generation of Beginners became more convinced the sailors planned to steal their remaining gold. They started building the wall higher. They filled the gate with stones because they feared outsiders would use it to enter their village. The Beginners now called themselves the Wallers.

"With each generation, the number of Wallers grew. Since the wall was now too large to move, the Wallers had to build more houses inside the wall. Houses were built on top of the gardens and in the parks where the Beginners' children once played. Eventually, only narrow paths were left between the Wallers' houses.

"When there was no room in the village to build new houses, the Wallers started adding second, then third, then fourth stories to their homes to accommodate the additional people being born in the village. Each time a house was built taller, the people behind the new house were forced to build additional levels to their homes to keep their view of the sea. These villagers became known as the Tallers.

"As the Tallers built the houses higher, they also had to build the wall higher to keep the highest houses protected from the outsiders." Darko finished the history of his village by saying, "That is where we are today. We are the fourth generation of Tallers. Our village has never been invaded. We have remained safe for hundreds of years. If we must build a roof over the entire village to save us from threats in the sky, we will have to give our generation a name too. What name can we give ourselves when we can no longer see the sky?"

Sofia, who traveled throughout the world, had never heard of a village like this one before. "Your fear of everything has made you prisoners in your own homes. You live on a beautiful island you have never explored. Your children grow up without running through open fields or chasing butterflies. You're afraid of one man with a donkey. That is no way to live."

Manuela addressed Sofia sadly, "How can we change when this life is all we have ever known?"

"First," Sofia responded, "you need to tear down the wall of fear inside your hearts. Then you need to tear down the wall of stone surrounding your village. I can help you tear down the wall of stone, but you'll need to help each other to rid yourselves of the walls around your hearts."

Darko addressed the people on the balcony. "The history of our people has been kept a secret for generations. I don't think we should make such a big decision without discussing it with everyone. It's clear we can't protect ourselves from a dragon. But this life is all we have ever known." Darko asked Ebby and Sofia to return the next day to give them time to decide what they would do.

Sofia and Ebby flew back to the field where Alotta Burrotta was waiting for them. She rushed to meet them, curious about what they had learned. Alotta shook her head in astonishment when they told her the history of the village. "Do you think the Beginners were the same people aboard the shipwreck you found?"

"It seems likely, but there are many shipwrecks on the bottom of the Big Sea," Sofia pointed out. "If it was the Beginners' ship, they went from being brave adventurers to people living in fear on the edge of a cliff behind a wall."

That night, after Ebby curled up next to Alotta and fell asleep, Sofia flew away into the darkness.

CHAPTER TWENTY-FOUR

Bringing Down the Wall

(In which Sofia helps bring down the wall with the help of the Tallers.)

Sofia was staring at the wall when Ebby woke the next morning. She did not realize Sofia had flown away during the night and had only just returned. Alotta broke open a pomegranate with her teeth and gave it to Ebby to eat. Ebby was surprised how sweet, juicy, and crunchy it was. After she finished it, she was ready to return to the village with Sofia.

There were no guards standing on the wall when they flew over it and landed on Darko's roof. They approached the edge together. The balcony was filled with villagers laughing and talking. More people lined the narrow paths surrounding the building. They grew silent when they saw Sofia's head extending over the roof.

Darko and Manuela greeted Sofia and Ebby warmly. Darko announced that the villagers agreed to accept Sofia's help to remove the wall. The discussion lasted late into the evening. Many were frightened something would happen if the wall was not there to protect them. Darko revealed the entire history of the village to them as set forth in the Book of Pages. He started with the shipwreck and told them everything he knew about the Beginners, the Wallers, and the Tallers. The records showed the wall was approached only once during all that time. It was a report he himself wrote about one man and one donkey arriving at the wall a few years earlier. Nothing had happened before or since, other than the arrival of a dragon and an Elusive Baby Bunny the day before, which he promptly added to the Book of Pages. Together the villagers concluded it would be worse to build a roof over the entire village than it would be to remove the wall and face their fears.

When Darko finished speaking, Sofia addressed the crowd with her sweet voice. "You have within each of you the power to push fear away. I can help you tear down the wall that surrounds your village, but first I will need your help to tear down the wall that surrounds your hearts. You have to open your hearts and think about what makes you the happiest."

The people of the village started thinking about what made them happy. Most of the Tallers thought about their children, wives, husbands, parents, or friends. Some were happiest watching the sun rise over the sea. A few of the Tallers thought about their favorite piece of gold jewelry. Not even one of them thought about the wall. It did not make them happy. It only made them more afraid. It did not matter to Sofia what made them happy; she just needed to sense their happiness.

Sofia turned away from the villagers and concentrated on the wall. As she stared at the wall, a sweet vibrating sound came from deep inside her heart. The sound got louder and louder. Ebby had never heard anything like it before. It sounded like Sofia's voice but deeper. Ebby felt like it wrapped her in pure love. She felt giddy.

The wall began to crumble before their eyes. The large

rocks, which had been used to build the wall, turned into dust. The sky above the village became bigger and bluer as layers of the wall fell away. The sound from Sofia's heart vibrated steadily through the air as more of the wall dissolved. The fields and forests, out of sight for hundreds of years, came into view. After several minutes the entire wall was gone as if it had never existed. Not even the dust was left. The vibrating sound from Sofia's chest faded away.

The Tallers started clapping and cheering. They laughed and hugged each other as the sunlight appeared where the wall had been. Tears of joy ran from their faces. Ebby ran to Sophia and gave her the biggest hug a little baby bunny had ever given anyone. Sofia picked Ebby up so she could see what was happening below.

The Tallers on the narrow paths below hurried toward the field where Alotta stood alone. She flicked her tail nervously from side to side as the crowd came towards her. Children ran over and reached out shyly to pet her. They had never seen a donkey before. She was soft and friendly. Alotta brayed joyfully, thrilled at all the attention she received.

Darko, Manuela, and the others on the balcony made their way down the stairs. When they reached the field, they stared at the bright colors of the trees, grass, and flowers. The trees were full of lemons, oranges, olives, and pomegranates. No living Taller except the guards on the wall had ever seen a tree before, and they thought all fruit came from the heavy cloth bags the sailors brought. Darko walked over to a tree and picked the biggest pomegranate he could reach and handed it to Manuela. Her face lit up with joy as she broke it open and tasted the sweet juice inside.

Sofia and Ebby flew down from the roof to join them. They watched happily as the Tallers explored their island for the first time. After spending several hours picking and eating the fruit from the trees, smelling the flowers in the field, and enjoying all the new experiences their island had to offer, the villagers paused to look at their bleak, crowded village. No windows faced the field because the wall had blocked the view. Darko talked with the other Tallers about rearranging the village to enjoy this side of the island as well.

"What do you think we should call ourselves now?" Darko asked Ebby and Sofia. "The Smallers? The No-Wallers?"

"You should call yourselves something splendid that makes you smile every time you hear it," Ebby said.

Ebby knew Sofia was remarkable in every way, but she did not understand how she was able to make the wall go away. When they were alone later that evening Ebby asked, "How did you do it, Sofia?"

"To be honest," Sofia replied, "I was worried I would never be able to take the wall down by myself. It was so big. Fear had kept the Beginners, Wallers, and Tallers prisoners behind a wall of their own making for hundreds of years. Each stone in the wall represented someone's fear at some time during their lives. The stones at the bottom of the wall placed there by the Beginners were soon covered by the stones of fear placed on top by the Wallers. The stones of fear placed by the Wallers were then covered by the Tallers' fears. Even if I took one stone away at a time it would take years. In the meantime, new fears could arise at any time and the villagers could rebuild the wall. I knew the villagers had to be part of the wall's destruction for it to work.

"I thought of my grandfather, Seamus. He was always able to help me find the answers to the hardest questions. After you and Alotta fell asleep, I flew back to the Land of Dragons to ask him how I could help the villagers.

"My grandfather had seen many walls in his worldly travels but none quite as drastic as the Tallers' wall. The Tallers' wall was not built to keep real danger out. The Beginners, Wallers, and Tallers were never attacked by the sailors or anyone else. It was their own fear that caused them to build the wall. The only way to demolish such a huge wall was for the villagers to overcome their fear. They had to want to get rid of it.

"He reminded me that baby dragons can break out of our diamond eggshells just by using the power of our hearts. Surely, he reasoned, an adult dragon could harness the power of thousands of hearts to break down a wall. The key was every villager would have to let go of their own fear at the same time for it to work.

"I know happiness is stronger than fear. I thought the only way to get rid of the wall was for every villager to think of something that made them happy. Once they were thinking about what made them happy, I could channel those feelings to destroy the wall. My grandfather always told me I could do anything with kindness and love. He thought my plan could work. I flew back to Zidani just moments before you woke up. I wasn't sure what would happen until the wall started disappearing."

Ebby was so proud Sofia figured out how to dissolve the wall. "Your grandfather was right. You can conquer fear with love and kindness."

They stayed on Zidani for several more days to help the

169

Tallers plan their new village. The villagers agreed to tear down the tallest buildings and build new houses all over the island. Each house would have a large yard for the children and fields to grow fruits and vegetables. Darko announced his house, which was the tallest in the village, would be the first to be taken down.

It was time for Ebby and Sofia to leave on their next adventure. They said goodbye to Alotta, who was now the most popular and beloved donkey there ever was. As they stood in the field, all the villagers gathered to thank Sofia and Ebby for freeing them from the wall and their fear. Darko approached Sofia. "We met last night and agreed to name our village *Sofia* in your honor. As Ebby suggested, it will make us smile and think of you every time we hear it." Darko kissed Sofia on her cheek and stepped back.

Manuela then walked up to Ebby. "Magnificent little Ebby, you have taught us it doesn't matter how big or small you are if

you have a big heart. Your heart is as big as a dragon's. We will forever teach our children about Ebby, the Elusive Baby Bunny who came and taught us that love is stronger than hatred and friends are more valuable than enemies. We know you can't stay because you are an Elusive Baby Bunny and want to see everything and go everywhere. We wish you many happy journeys." After saying their final goodbyes, Sofia picked up Ebby and they flew away.

The villagers had traded most of their remaining gold treasure to purchase the food they were unloading when Sofia first flew over them. When taking down his house, Darko found the large pile of diamond tears Sofia left on his roof. They would never have to worry about the treasure again.

Many years later, Sofia flew over the village named after her. They had not rebuilt the wall and the sight of the village made her heart sing.

CHAPTER TWENTY-FIVE

Sofia's Triumphant Return to Slune

(In which Ebby and Sofia return to visit Slune.)

Ebby and Sofia cherished the time they spent on Zidani Island. They helped an entire village free themselves from fear and start a new life while making lots of friends in the process. Now it was time for Ebby to help Sofia.

Ebby chose Slune as their next destination because she knew it was important to Sofia. Sofia promised her grandfather she would tell him what it was like, but when she visited Slune years earlier it had been a complete disaster. The people were terrified of her and ran away. She left in shame and was too embarrassed to tell her grandfather about the visit. Sofia always wanted to go back and show the people of Slune she was not a threat, but she did not know how to do that without scaring them again. Ebby knew Sofia would be welcomed to Slune with warmth and friendship this time, and it would replace the horrible memory of her first visit.

As Sofia flew back over the Land of Stones, Ebby watched islands of every shape and size pass below her. Ebby supposed each island had a story, just like Zidani. It would take a lifetime just to visit all the Stone Islands and she still had the rest of the world to explore. No wonder Elusive Baby Bunnies were hard to find! She wanted to see and do everything there was to see and do. There was no time to sit around and wait for someone to find her.

Sofia landed in a forest a short distance from Slune. Ebby wanted to avoid another dreadful visit for her plan to help Sofia be successful. Ebby thought it would be best to go into town alone and bring Nikola back to meet Sofia. Nikola could then gently introduce Sofia to the people of Slune in a way that would not scare them.

Ebby went to the dock where she had first met Nikola, but it was empty. There were no fishermen or villagers anywhere, and all the boats were tied up at the dock. Since it was still early, she thought she might find him playing Hide and Seek with his friends before school. She went to the paths along the rivers and waterfalls hoping to find him there. No one was on the paths or in the main square. In fact, she did not see anyone at all. That is odd, she thought to herself.

Although Nikola usually played outside all day when he was not in school, Ebby thought he might be at home reading or helping his parents, so she headed to his house. The house was quiet. The door was closed, and no smoke rose from the chimney. The window by the door was shut, but the curtains were pulled back.

She stood up on her back legs and knocked on the big wooden door with her front paw. It barely made any noise because her paw was so soft and fluffy. No one came to the door. She stood back from the house to see through the window. Lights were on inside so she knew someone was home. She found a little stick and put it between her front toes. Standing on her back legs she stretched as tall as she could to tap on the window with the stick, but the window was too high.

Ebby looked for something to stand on to reach the window but there was nothing big enough. She briefly thought about getting Sofia to help her. Then she imagined what Nikola's parents would do if a purple dragon as big as their house knocked on their door. This was not how Ebby wanted to introduce them to Sofia.

Ebby realized she had the power within herself to solve the problem, just as Rebby the Gallant had done in dislodging the huge boulder. She was settling on an easy answer while ignoring a slightly harder one. There are two things bunnies do exceptionally well: dig and jump. She put the stick in her mouth and ran as fast as she could for the window. At the last moment, just before she was going to hit the wall, she jumped as high as she could, and grabbing the stick from her mouth, hit the window. It made a tiny sound. Ebby stepped back and waited at the door expectantly. Nothing happened.

Not willing to give up, Ebby made another run at the window. This time she jumped even higher than the first time and struck the glass harder. It sounded like a small pebble hitting the window. Ebby dropped the stick and hurried back to the front door.

This time the door opened. Nikola's mother, Victoria, stuck her head out to see what had hit the window. The stick on the ground caught her attention and then she spotted Ebby. Victoria's eyes were red from crying. She managed to smile at the sight of Ebby and dabbed her eyes on her sleeve. "Oh, little Ebby, I am so relieved to see you! Something awful has happened to Nikola!"

CHAPTER TWENTY-SIX

Skrufty Fluffbottom

*(In which Ebby and Sofia join forces to save Nikola
with their new friend, Skrufty Fluffbottom.)*

Ebby's ears drooped when she heard something horrible had happened to Nikola. Her heart raced. "What happened to him? Where is he? Can I see him?" she asked rapidly, not pausing for Victoria to answer each question.

Victoria took a deep breath before telling Ebby what happened. "Nikola has had so much fun since you helped him make friends. He's no longer sad, and his grades are much better. Yesterday he and his friends were playing in the waterfalls behind the village. There is one large waterfall where two rivers join together before flowing into town. The boys found a way to go behind the waterfall and discovered a big cave. Close to the entry of the cave they found a marble statue covered in moss. It was probably made by the ancient people a thousand years ago. There are lots of stories throughout the Land of Stones about finding treasures hidden by the ancient people who used to live here." Ebby knew about this because of her own explorations in the forest near Roveen with Soto and the treasures in the shipwreck.

"The boys started to go farther into the cave, but it was too dark and wet. They came back and told us what they found. We were so excited and proud of them. We were also relieved they didn't try to explore the cave on their own. The Land of Stones is full of caves. Some of the caves go for miles underground and are so large entire buildings would fit in them. It's easy to get lost or hurt even if you're a cave expert." Victoria dabbed her eyes.

"We met last night in the main square to discuss investigating the cave further. The village elders reminded us that although it was possible we would find ancient treasure, cave explorations could be risky. You need proper lights, ropes, warm clothing, and strong shoes to safely explore caves. The boys already knew the cave was dark and that water dripped from the ceilings. This would make it difficult to keep torches lit.

"The village elders asked for volunteers to explore the cave. Nikola raised his hand but his father and I said he was too young. Several older villagers volunteered to fetch the necessary equipment from a neighboring village and search the cave when they returned in a few days. Everyone agreed the search would have to wait until they returned. Nikola was upset he couldn't search the cave since he and his friends found it. He was certain there was treasure in the cave and didn't think it was fair someone else would find it.

"Last night we told him how proud we were that he found the cave. We told him he could explore anywhere he wanted when he was older but that it just wasn't safe. He went to bed early. We could tell he wasn't happy.

"I went to wake him for school this morning and he wasn't in bed. He left this note on his pillow. It says, 'I am going to explore the cave. I promise to be careful. I didn't find the purple sea dragon, but I will find something in the cave that will make everyone remember me.' " Victoria burst out crying as she finished reading Nikola's note.

Between sobs she told Ebby everyone went to the cave to find Nikola, but he had not been found. The mouth of the cave was big, but as soon as they ventured in a short distance the cave became too dark and wet to see. They called for him but heard no response. "We desperately want to find him but we don't have torches or ropes yet. Between having to pass behind the waterfall and the water dripping from the ceiling, we can't keep the candles lit. We're afraid that anyone trying to find Nikola will get lost too. I came back to the house to see if we have anything here that could be used to help find Nikola. I never expected to find you here! Is there anything you can do to help?"

Ebby was worried about Nikola and did not want Victoria to cry. "I came back to Slune with Sofia, the magical purple sea dragon. Sofia will know what to do."

Victoria was astounded. "Sofia is here? Please take me to meet her." They hurried to the hillside where Ebby had left Sofia.

While Ebby was in Slune trying to track down Nikola, Sofia was trying to track down a Dragon Tree in the forest above the town. She was hungry and still a bit tired from the commotion on Zidani Island. The only food Sofia liked to eat came from Dragon Trees, which were rare and difficult to find. Just as she was about to give up on finding one, she heard a small branch creak on a tree limb above her head. She came eye to eye with the furriest, puffiest squirrel she ever saw.

"Why, hello there, little guy," Sofia said in her magical voice. The squirrel froze mid-jump and almost fell off the branch. His ears and tail twitched rapidly. He blinked his eyes several times as if he was trying to convince his brain he was looking directly into the eyes of a purple dragon.

Sofia smiled. "I'm sorry I startled you. My name is Sofia. Do you know where I can find a Dragon Tree so I can get something to eat?"

The squirrel kept his back legs where they were but stretched his front legs as far forward as he could. He lifted his head to get as close to Sofia as possible but still be able to get away if necessary. He had never seen a purple dragon in his forest before. His nose twitched as he sniffed her. She smelled like happiness. He knew instantly he was not in any danger.

"Hi, Sofia! I'm Skrufty Fluffbottom. Welcome to my forest. I know everything there is to know about this place. I'm quite certain you won't find a Dragon Tree here, but there's one growing on the mountain by the old castle in the clouds. If you're hungry, I have a huge collection of forest nuts and other tasty niblets. I would be honored to share them with you."

Sofia was touched. She knew squirrels spent almost all year storing food for the long, cold winter months. "That's sweet of you Skrufty, but nuts get stuck between my teeth. I can wait until after I've visited Slune to fly to the Dragon Tree by the castle."

"What are you doing here? I've never seen you in my forest before. Sometimes I forget where I hid my nuts, but I'm pretty sure I would have remembered seeing a dragon like you. Are you lost?"

Sofia told Skrufty about her first visit to Slune and how it had ended so poorly. "My grandfather told me there's no other

village like this in the world. I want to explore it and meet the people who live here and show them they don't need to be afraid of me. I'm here with my friend Ebby. She's an Elusive Baby Bunny. She went to town to bring back a little boy named Nikola whom she met on her first visit to Slune."

Skrufty, who had not traveled around the world like Sofia, thought all villages were built on top of rivers and waterfalls. He had no idea Slune was unusual. "You mean there are villages that aren't built on top of rivers and don't have waterfalls running through them?"

Sofia shook her head and laughed. "There is no other place

quite like Slune. And, to be honest, I've never seen a fluffier squirrel than you. What a mystical this place is!"

Sofia's compliment thrilled Skrufty. He came from a long line of Fluffbottoms and was proud of his fluffiness.

"Well, I need to get back to our meeting place," Sofia said. "I'm sure Ebby is on her way back with Nikola. Would you like to come and meet Ebby?"

Skrufty was curious. He never met an Elusive Baby Bunny before. His parents told him about the incredible adventures of Elusive Baby Bunnies, but Skrufty did not know they were real. He thought his parents just told him about Elusive Baby Bunnies so he would be nice to everyone he met. But then, until he met Sofia, he did not think dragons were real either. "If Ebby is anything like the bedtime stories my parents told me about Elusive Baby Bunnies, I definitely want to meet her! I can also give you a tour of the areas outside the village. I know every nook and cranny around here."

Sofia walked back to the clearing. Skrufty jumped from tree to tree high above her head. They arrived just as Ebby was approaching with a woman.

Victoria stopped and stared when she saw Sofia coming through the trees. She put her hand on her chest and breathed deeply. Ebby ran up to Sofia. "This is Victoria. She is Nikola's mother. Something terrible has happened to him."

Ebby explained the situation to Sofia. When Ebby reached the part in the story about Nikola's note, Victoria burst into tears. Sofia was so moved a big tear fell from her eye.

"What can we do, Sofia?" Ebby asked. "How can we find Nikola? The cave is too small for you. I could go into the cave to find him, but I don't know my way around. I don't know how I could safely bring him back if I found him."

Just as Ebby asked Sofia what they could do to save Nikola, Skrufty jumped down from a tree and approached Ebby. "Hi, Ebby, I'm Skrufty Fluffbottom. It's a true pleasure to meet a real live Elusive Baby Bunny! I can take you to the cave. That's where I store my nuts. I'll help you find him."

"You'll help us find my son, Mr. Fluffbottom?" Victoria asked gratefully.

"Of course, I will! And please call me Skrufty. My parents always told me to ask myself, 'What would an Elusive Baby Bunny do?' The answer was always the same: 'Do what is kind and helpful.'"

Ebby was tickled. Skrufty said the exact same thing her own mother told her as she left Fluffle Valley: "Be kind and helpful." It was exceptional advice.

"How will you be able to lead him out if you find him?" Victoria asked wringing her hands together. "It's dark and dangerous in the cave. He could hit his head or fall into a hole."

Sofia smiled and picked up the diamond tear she shed a few minutes earlier. "I have just the thing for you." She blew softly on the tear and it started glowing. She blew on it again. The light shone brighter and brighter from inside the tear until it was like a miniature sun. "This should last a few hours."

CHAPTER TWENTY-SEVEN

Into the Labyrinth

(In which Ebby and Skrufty Fluffbottom venture
deep underground in search of Nikola.)

Ebby, Skrufty, and Victoria were fascinated by the glowing diamond dragon tear Sofia held. It shined so brightly it almost dulled the light from the sun. Sofia turned to Ebby. "I know you and Skrufty can see in the dark, but this should provide sufficient light for Nikola when you find him. The light will not be affected if it gets wet. You will know it is losing power when the light starts turning a purplish hue."

Ebby stood and held her front paws out for the glowing tear. Although it was tiny in Sofia's hand, it was huge in Ebby's front paws. Ebby knew she would be able to travel easier through the cave on all four feet. She set the tear on top of her head and wriggled her ears around until it fit comfortably between them. She then squeezed her ears tightly around it. She hopped around a bit to make sure it would not fall. It did not budge. Once they found Nikola, he could hold it to find his way back out. "Let's go!"

Victoria walked toward the cave, followed by Ebby and Sofia. Skrufty preferred to jump from tree to tree, so he stayed high above their heads. They walked through the woods until they reached a path alongside a river that flowed through the village. Victoria turned on the path and walked upriver towards the waterfall.

The distant sound of the waterfall grew louder as they approached until it became a deafening roar. The air was full of mist as the water cascaded down the sheer rock wall of the mountain. The side of the mountain was covered with bright green ferns and other plants constantly watered by the falls. A few exceptionally sturdy trees grew out of the cracks in the rock face of the cliff. Ebby did not know how Nikola and his friends were able to climb the cliff to get behind the waterfall. It was scary even for an Elusive Baby Bunny.

The villagers from Slune were gathered at the bottom of the waterfall. They looked up anxiously as if they expected to see Nikola poke his head out from behind the falling water at any moment. They did not see Ebby or the others coming up the path. Victoria called out to the villagers to get their attention. Nikola's father, Alex, turned around to face the odd group of rescuers. A big smile came to his face when he

recognized Ebby, followed instantly by sheer terror when he saw Sofia behind her. Victoria sped up to reach her husband so she could tell him about Sofia and Ebby. With the roar of the waterfall, Victoria had to yell their rescue plan into his ear.

The villagers turned around at the same time as Alex and saw Victoria hurrying towards them. They mistakenly thought she was running away from the big purple dragon. They looked around for a place to hide, just as the villagers on Zidani Island did when they first saw Sofia flying overhead. In the panic, two of the villagers stumbled backwards and fell into the river. They were swept underneath the waterfall. The water swirled powerfully, and Sofia could see they were in trouble. Without hesitating, Sofia dove in and swam directly towards the two villagers. She carefully grabbed one in each of her clawed hands before flying out of the water. She landed next to the other villagers and set the soaking wet couple down gently as they shivered and hugged each other. They backed away from Sofia towards the safety of the other villagers, who had watched the entire startling rescue.

Victoria loudly announced that Sofia came to help find Nikola and that they should not be afraid of her. Sofia shook the water off her body, which drenched everyone there. Alex shrieked from the shock of the cold water hitting him. Everyone chuckled nervously half expecting Sofia to eat him.

Sofia was embarrassed. This was not how she hoped to meet the villagers of Slune. "I am so sorry I startled you and drenched your clothes," she said in her magically sweet voice. "I was hoping to blend in a little better this time, but it is difficult blending in when you're a purple dragon."

Alex brushed the water from his arms and walked to Sofia. "Sofia, I don't think you could blend in even if there were 100 other purple dragons. You are extraordinary! Thank you for rescuing our friends and for coming to save Nikola. Welcome to Slune. I hope you are able to enjoy your visit once he's rescued." He then bent over to give Ebby a big kiss on her wet forehead but was blinded by the tear she held there with her ears. "What is this?"

Ebby explained what the tear was and how it was made. "Skrufty and I will use it to bring Nikola out of the cave safely."

"Who's Skrufty?" Alex asked.

Just then, Skrufty jumped out of a nearby tree and landed a short distance from Ebby. He skipped and jumped up to the crowd of villagers. "I'm Skrufty Fluffbottom." Skrufty's big fluffy tail twitched rapidly from side to side, making him appear even bigger and fluffier than he was. "I've been storing my nuts in the cave for years. We'll find your son and bring him home to you." The villagers gathered around the rescuers and wished Ebby and Skrufty luck in finding Nikola.

Although it would be easy for Skrufty to climb to the cave, Ebby was not used to going straight up the side of a cliff. She was worried about dropping Sofia's tear. To make their journey easier, Sofia picked up Ebby and Skrufty. "Please take a step back," she asked the villagers before opening her wings and pushing off the ground. She flew close to the waterfall until she found the cave ledge. Darting through the water, she landed at the mouth of the cave behind the waterfall.

Sofia set them down on the wet ground. The rocky ledge was covered with moss and puddles of water. The glow from Sofia's diamond tear lit up the entrance. The cave entrance was not big enough for Sofia. She would not be able to go any farther. "Be careful, you two. If you need me, just hold the tear next to your heart and think of me."

Ebby kissed Sofia on her wet nose and exclaimed, "Nikola needs us, Skrufty. Let's go get him!"

Skrufty led Ebby inside the cave. He hopped right past the old statue the boys had found as if it were just another

rock. He never understood why humans carved rocks to look like themselves. It made as much sense to him as carving a stone nut. Before they went farther, Skrufty explained the underground maze they were about to enter.

"The cave consists of four separate caverns that go deep into the mountain." Skrufty's tail twitched with excitement as he spoke. "I keep my nuts in the second cavern. I rarely go to the first cavern on the left. It's not at all suitable for storing nuts. Underground springs make it too wet plus it's full of stone men and women and other things the ancient people left on the floor. It's not very big so we can check there first." They made their way to the opening of the first cavern. It was full of marble statues and large wooden trunks. A few of the trunks had rotted and broken apart at the seams, revealing gold and silver objects inside. It resembled the treasure Ebby saw at the shipwreck.

Ebby called out for Nikola. Her voice echoed off the walls. She could see all the way to the end of the cavern. Nikola was not here. As Ebby turned to leave, the glow of the diamond tear sparkled against a gold ring set with blue and white stones lying on the ground. Ebby remembered Nikola's note promising to bring something back from the cave. She hopped over and picked it up. It was too cumbersome to carry the whole time they searched for Nikola. She took it back to the outer entrance of the cave and set it on a rock to retrieve later.

Next, they went to the mouth of the second cavern. The opening to this cavern was only a few feet high. It would be barely big enough for Nikola to crawl through. "This is my place. It's the real treasure!" Skrufty led Ebby inside. After passing through the small opening, the second cavern became much bigger. The floor was covered with piles of walnuts reaching all the way to the ceiling.

"I keep my nuts here because it stays cool and dry. I can store them here for years without them going bad. This is the only place I would want to explore if I just found this cave," Skrufty said matter-of-factly. "You could live here for years without ever going hungry! The first cavern is full of silly stuff you could never eat." Ebby could not argue with Skrufty's logic.

Skrufty sniffed the air to see if he could detect the scent of a human boy. All he could smell were his delicious walnuts. Ebby did not see Nikola's footprints on the cavern floor. "He's not in this one either. Let's go to the next one."

"The third cavern is wet and goes deep into the mountain," Skrufty explained. "I never went far into this cavern because I could hear water in the distance. Moisture is bad for nuts."

The entrance to this cavern was bigger than the one where Skrufty kept his nuts. After taking thirty steps the cavern opened into a large underground chamber. The light from Sofia's tear illuminated hundreds of rock formations hanging from the ceiling. Some extended from the ceiling to the ground like large columns. Others hung partway down and ended in sharp pointed tips. Some rocks grew up out of the ground, reaching upwards. Ebby had never seen anything like it.

Water dripped everywhere; it dripped from cracks in the ceiling and filled small puddles in the cavern floor. It dripped off the rocks dangling from the ceiling. Some of the drops landed on top of the pointy rocks that grew up from the ground. Although Ebby could see the rough outlines of these rocks as her eyes grew accustomed to the darkness, she took

Sofia's tear from between her ears and held it out in front of her. The light bounced off the wet rock formations, creating shadows everywhere in the chamber.

Skrufty stood up on his back legs and sniffed the air hoping to catch Nikola's scent, but the air was too damp. Ebby did not see any footprints on the wet ground. She could not even see where she and Skrufty had just stepped.

Ebby called out to Nikola. The sound of her voice not only bounced off the walls, but off the rock formations as well. The competing echoes of her voice joined the sound of the water dripping making it impossible for her to hear whether Nikola responded. She called out his name again. Skrufty turned his head towards the back of the cavern and listened intently. Despite bunnies and squirrels having sensitive hearing, neither of them could hear anything that sounded like a boy.

"We'd better explore this one," Ebby said. "If he's in this cavern, it will be difficult for him to find his way out."

Ebby placed the diamond tear back on her head and wrapped her ears around it. The ground was slippery and uneven as they hopped, skipped, and jumped from spot to spot, trying to avoid the water that came from everywhere. They were soon so far into the cavern they could no longer see the light from the entrance. The floor slowly sloped downward. After a few minutes their feet were so wet they stopped trying to avoid the water covering the ground.

The large chamber dwindled down into a small tunnel. They followed the tunnel deeper into the mountain. Soon, Ebby heard the sound of rushing water ahead of her. As they got closer to the sound, they felt a slight breeze blowing against their whiskers. The tunnel ended, and they found themselves inside an enormous underground chamber. There was enough space for Sofia to fly in here, Ebby thought to herself.

There was a waterfall at the far end of the chamber that was bigger than the waterfall outside the cave. The water fell straight down from far above before crashing with a roar into a lake that churned and frothed endlessly. Rocks smoothed by the constant flow of water surrounded the lake. The lake narrowed into a channel at the far end of the chamber, and an underground river took the water somewhere out of sight. The light from Sofia's tear caused a rainbow to occur in the mist created by the waterfall. Ebby wished Sofia could see this breathtakingly beautiful place.

Ebby and Skrufty poked around the chamber hoping to spot Nikola, but there was no sign of him. Skrufty jumped to the edge of the pool. Without warning something came to the surface of the cold, dark water.

CHAPTER TWENTY-EIGHT

Solomon of the Underground

(In which Ebby and Skrufty make a special discovery.)

The Waterfall Caves

Skrufty jumped straight up launching himself away from the water's edge in one fluid movement. Upon landing, he flipped around midair and turned to Ebby. His eyes were wide, and he started to say something, but all he could do was stammer. "Th-th-th-er-ere i-i-is s-s-so-so-some-th-th-ing i-i-in t-t-the w-w-a-at-t-ter!" He pointed at the spot where he had just been standing.

Ebby did not know what startled Skrufty. She hopped over to the edge of the lake. Skrufty stood frozen in the spot where he landed. The warm glow from Sofia's tear lit up the water. Ebby peered in and a nose emerged from under the water's surface a few inches from her nose. Ebby leaned in towards the nose. Ebby sniffed it. The nose sniffed back. Ebby sniffed it again. The nose sniffed her again. Ebby smiled. She had found a new friend.

"Hello, my name is Ebby. That was Skrufty Fluffbottom. I hope he didn't scare you. Please forgive us for coming into your home without bringing you anything. We didn't know anyone lived in this cavern or I would have brought you some yummy yellow flowers. What's your name?"

The creature crawled unhurriedly out of the lake. He lifted his head out of the water first, followed by his long slender body. He was nearly twice as long as Skrufty's tail, but not at all fluffy. He did not have any hair on his body. Ebby took a few steps back to give him some room. His body was thin, smooth, and brightly colored in shades of blues and greens, which sparkled from the diamond tear light. His two front legs were close to his head with three toes on each foot. Two back legs grew close to the end of his tail. His back feet had only two toes each. He climbed up onto the smooth flat rock. Bright red fins stuck out of the side of his head. Although he was not big, he reminded Ebby of Sofia. "Are you a baby dragon?" Ebby asked.

"Hello, Ebby," he said in a slow and deliberate manner. "My name is Solomon. No, I am not a baby dragon. I am an olm. You smell most unusual to me. Where are you from? What is that thing on your head? It feels strange on my skin."

His eyes were closed tightly, but he could somehow sense the light coming from Sofia's tear.

Feeling less skittish than he was at first, Skrufty edged his way back and stood next to Ebby, his tail flitting around as he sat on his rear haunches examining the unusual creature.

"It's very nice to meet you, Solomon. We come from the land outside of the cave. We're looking for a boy named Nikola who's lost. The glowing light on my head is a diamond dragon tear from my friend, Sofia. It's for Nikola because he can't see in the dark. Without the tear he won't be able to find his way out of the cave."

She moved her ears so they would cover the light coming from Sofia's tear. She did not want to make Solomon feel uncomfortable. She and Skrufty blinked several times to get adjusted to the darkness. Solomon was no longer blue and green when they were able to see him. His skin was now a pinkish color. Ebby moved her ears slightly to expose the light again, and Solomon's skin went back to being blue, green, and glowing. She covered the diamond tear, and his skin became pink again. It must have something to do with the dragon light, Ebby concluded.

"What do you mean there is a land outside of the cave?" Solomon asked.

Solomon was not aware of the Land of Stones just as the villagers on Zidani Island did not know about the world outside of their walled village. Ebby did not know anything about the world outside of her fluffle either until she stood on Chip's log. She was not sure how to describe a world so different from this cave to someone who could not see.

"Have you ever had a visitor from the outside world before?" Ebby asked.

"No. I have never been with anyone other than my family. Only olms live here. Until I met the two of you, I did not know anyone else existed." Ebby could not imagine never having seen the sun or moon, grass or yummy yellow flowers, dragons, foxes or roosters.

"How do you feed yourself? I don't see any grass, flowers,

or even nuts like Skrufty eats," Ebby said.

Solomon replied, "There is usually enough for us to eat in the water. The food comes to us from the waterfall. But we can go a long time without eating if we need to. One time I went without eating for ten years." Ebby had never heard anything like that before. She didn't know how long ten years was, but it sounded like a long time. She needed to eat several times a day.

"Do you ever get lonely?" Skrufty asked.

"I am never alone. I live here with my family and friends."

Ebby and Skrufty were mesmerized by the way Solomon spoke and moved. Each motion took considerable effort. They asked him more questions about his life in this underground world.

"Olms can live for a long time. My grandfather lived to be almost one hundred years old. If there is not enough food, we stay still and save our energy for when we have food again. We can only be out of the water for a short period of time."

Ebby did not know creatures like Solomon existed. He was so beautiful, delicate, and graceful. "I wish we had more time to get to know you, Solomon, but we need to find Nikola. He is alone and probably scared. There are four underground caverns in this mountain. We already searched the first two caverns and this is the third. Can you help us find him?"

Solomon replied that although he had eyes, he could not see with them. He instead relied on his nose and ears to find food and make his way around the cavern. He lifted his head up high and smelled the air. He could smell Ebby and Skrufty. "You smell sweet. I don't know what a boy smells like, but I cannot smell anything other than the two of you. I will try to hear whether he is moving in the cavern. I did not hear anything unusual before you showed up, but the waterfall usually drowns out most sounds when I am underwater."

Solomon lifted his head again. He turned his head one way, then the other. Ebby and Skrufty held their breath, not wanting to make even the slightest sound. Solomon spread his toes apart and stood still. His toes were highly sensitive and could sense movement in the ground. After what felt like a lifetime, Solomon spoke. "I am certain there is no one else here other than us."

Ebby and Skrufty let out their breath. "He must be in the fourth cavern!"

"I can take you there. I have never left this cavern before, but I will help you find your friend."

CHAPTER TWENTY-NINE

The Olm Chain and the Fourth Cavern

(In which Solomon and his family help Ebby and Skrufty rescue Nikola.)

The Waterfall Caves

S olomon wanted to tell his family where he was going so they would not worry about him. He climbed to the edge of the rock and dove into the water without making a splash.

Ebby and Skrufty could not believe their good fortune. Neither of them had any idea there were creatures who lived their entire lives in deep underground caves. Ebby's home was underground too, but this was deep underground. Ebby now understood there was life everywhere she went. Every place was someone's home.

Solomon came back with about thirty other olms. "They want to help search for Nikola too." Solomon pointed to an olm who stood close to him. "This is my cousin, Salaman. He visits the fourth cavern often because his wife is from there. He knows a shortcut."

Salaman addressed Ebby and Skrufty. "There is an opening in the wall which separates the two caverns. The opening is underwater so we will have to swim through it to get to the other side. It is close to where the river empties into a dark hole and the current is fast. We do not know where the river flows or how deep it goes once it disappears. Nothing that went down the hole was ever seen again." Salaman spoke in a deliberate and unhurried manner that was somehow soothing even though he was issuing a grave warning to them.

It was easy for an olm to slip in between the rocks and the swift flowing water. Olms could breathe underwater and were used to moving through the cavern. It would be much more difficult for a bunny and squirrel to do it. Salaman said the olms would form a chain for Ebby and Skrufty to hold onto as they went through the underwater opening into the fourth cavern.

Ebby, fearless as always, thought this was a great idea. It would take much less time to use Salaman's shortcut through the underwater passage than go all the way back out to the entrance of the cave. The diamond tear was still glowing brightly, but the light was starting to turn slightly purple. Sofia had advised Ebby that the light would only last a couple of hours and would turn purple as it dimmed.

Skrufty was a little worried about diving into the cold, dark water. He spent all his time jumping around in trees, not swimming underwater. But if there was one thing Skrufty was good at, it was holding on to things with his long, strong fingers. He could walk backwards and forwards up the steepest, slipperiest surface without missing a step. If the olms were willing to help complete strangers, he was going to be there too. "Let's go find Nikola!" Skrufty announced.

Salaman led the contingent of olms through the water to the end of the lake. Ebby and Skrufty followed on the ground. The flow of the water quickened as the broad lake narrowed into the tight channel and formed a river. The river tossed and rolled as it cascaded into a dark hole with a deafening roar. The olms swam to the edge of the river and climbed up onto the rocks. The light from Sofia's tear glowed over the olms, turning their bodies into a bright patchwork of blues and greens. Each one was beautiful and different.

Solomon addressed Ebby and Skrufty. "We are going to form a chain underwater. We will each grab the tail of the olm in front of us. We will not let go until you are safely in the fourth cavern on the other side of the opening. Hold on to us and move forward as quickly as you can. Whatever you do, do not let go."

The olms slid underwater one by one until only Solomon remained on the shore. He turned to Ebby and asked if she was ready. Ebby nodded and drew in a big breath. Solomon ducked under the water and grabbed the tail of the closest olm while anchoring himself to the rocky shore with his rear legs. Ebby clenched Sofia's tear with her ears as tightly as she could and jumped into the water. The water was cold, but her thick, soft bunny hair kept her warm. She grabbed Solomon with her front paws and started moving down the chain of olms. She gripped each one tightly but carefully as she moved. When she was completely underwater, she could only hear the roar of the water all around her. She was grateful Sofia and Soto taught her how to swim.

Sofia's tear glowed underwater. It faintly lit up the olm chain. The olms gripped one another with their tiny feet firmly wrapped around the tail of the olm in front of them. The "chain of olms" extended through a small opening in the wall and continued into the other side. Ebby carefully worked her way down the olms, making sure not to squeeze them too tightly.

Ebby felt the pull of the current against her body. It tugged on her, forcing her in a sideways direction. She gritted her teeth and clenched her ears tightly around the diamond tear. She did not want to lose it when they were so close to finding Nikola. She knew if the tear slipped out of her ears it would be gone forever. Olm by olm she moved forward. She finally made it to the opening in the cavern wall. The hole was barely big enough for her to get through. Once she squeezed through the opening, she pulled herself up the olm chain until she found herself out of the water on the other side. Drawing a big breath, she saw she was in a small underground lake in the fourth cavern.

She swam to the edge of the lake and climbed out. As soon as she was on solid ground, she shook the water off her body. Skrufty popped up a few seconds later. He was almost unrecognizable. His tail was soaking wet, and it looked more like an olm than a fluffy squirrel tail. He swam to the shore and leaped onto the ground. He shook himself and his tail so rapidly he was completely dry and fluffy within seconds.

"Wow! That was something I never imagined I would do!"

he exclaimed.

The olms let go of each other and swam to the surface of the water. Solomon was the last one to pop up.

"Spread out," Solomon said to the other olms, "and if you find Nikola call out to the group." They silently scattered into the darkness of the fourth cavern.

Ebby sat up on her haunches and adjusted the tear between her ears again. This cavern was much smaller than the one they just left. Sofia would not be able to move around much in this one, let alone fly. It was also much quieter, almost silent. She could not hear the roar of the waterfall from the third cavern. The only water flowing in this cavern came from the small opening they just swam through. There were a lot of rock formations hanging from the ceiling and growing up out of the ground, but they were not as big as in the third cavern.

She held up Sofia's tear and called out to Nikola, hoping he would see the light. It was turning darker purple. Nikola did not respond. They were starting to run out of time. The olms returned and reported they had not heard or smelled anything. Ebby was becoming concerned.

"Do not be worried," Solomon said. "If he is here, we will find him."

Just then Salaman returned from seeing his wife's family who lived under rocks in the water. "My father-in-law smelled an unusual odor earlier today. He did not know what it was because he does not know what a boy smells like. He just knows he has never smelled anything like it before. I think it could be your friend."

Salaman led the way as they headed in the direction of the strange smell. The rescuers covered the cave floor as they moved together swiftly. No one made a sound. The cave climbed gradually upwards, and the path made several turns. There were a lot of places for a boy to get lost. Finally, after several more minutes of climbing uphill, Ebby spotted Nikola huddled in a ball against a big rock. He was shuddering in the cold and crying. Ebby imagined he was even sadder than the first time she saw him on the dock.

It was pitch black in the cavern and Nikola was not able to see or hear the olms approaching. Ebby loosened her ears from around the tear and let it light up the cave. She called out to Nikola as they rushed towards him. Nikola lifted his head to see who had called his name from the darkness in the cave.

First, all Nikola could see was a faint purple light bouncing up and down near the ground. As the light got closer, he noticed blue and green glowing creatures crawling towards him. Nikola yelled, "Cave Snakes!!!" He got ready to jump up and run away when he recognized Ebby holding the purple light. Ebby ran up to him and jumped onto his lap and into his opened arms. He sobbed as he hugged her. "Oh, Ebby! You came to rescue me! You are the best friend anyone could ever want. How did you find me?"

Ebby pointed to the group of rescuers. "Skrufty and the olms helped me find you. I could not have done it without them. This was the most fantastic game of Hide and Seek ever!"

Suddenly Nikola felt embarrassed. He was so relieved to be found, but now he was ashamed he had caused so much trouble in the first place. "I am so sorry, Ebby. I never should have tried to explore this cave by myself. I should have listened to my parents when they told me it was not safe. I just wanted to do something special and didn't think about the consequences." Nikola choked back tears. "It was fun until I got lost and turned around in the dark. I didn't know which way to go. I kept bumping into rocks and falling on the slippery floor. It was so scary. I didn't think I would ever be found."

Solomon spoke to Nikola. "I am glad we were able to help Ebby and Skrufty find you, but it was dangerous. Any of us, including Ebby, could have gotten hurt or lost forever. You should always think about what could happen to those who love you when you put yourself in danger. Now we need to get home before our families start worrying about us."

Ebby thanked Solomon and the other olms for their help. "If you ever want to visit the outside world, please let Skrufty know. He visits the second cavern all the time. He would love to show you around, and I would love to help him if I am here, but there's no knowing where I'll be."

Solomon smiled. It was funny to him that he could stay in the same place for ten years without moving a muscle and Ebby could not stay still for a moment. He headed back down into the cavern with his family in tow. Nikola yelled out his thanks and waved goodbye to them. His voice echoed through the chamber as he wiped the tears from his eyes.

Ebby watched as the olms slipped away into the darkness. She knew they had used a lot of energy to help her search for Nikola and hoped they would be all right. She would never forget their kindness in helping find Nikola.

Sofia's tear was getting dimmer as it turned a darker purple. Ebby knew she needed to get Nikola out of the cave quickly. "Nikola, this is Skrufty Fluffbottom. He'll help get us through the rest of this cave." She handed the tear to Nikola. "Take this and hold it up to light your way through the cave. Stay close to us. Skrufty and I can see in the dark and will warn you of any danger. We haven't been in this part of the cave before. But don't worry. No matter what happens, we won't leave you in here."

Nikola took the tear from Ebby. It was warm and felt magical to him, but he did not know what it was. "How did you find me in here if you haven't been this way before? Didn't you come through the cave opening by the waterfall?"

Ebby briefly mentioned how she and Skrufty entered the cavern through an underwater opening deeper inside the mountain. She started to talk about the olm chain, but the tear was getting dimmer. They were running out of time and Nikola would be in complete darkness again. "We need to go now. I'll answer all of your questions later." Ebby and Skrufty hurried towards the cave entrance with Nikola following close behind. Soon, they heard the far-off sound of the waterfall outside the cave.

Even though it was dim, Sofia's tear was still much brighter than Nikola's candle had been. Nikola saw large cracks in the floor, big deep holes full of water, and rocks dangling from the ceiling and growing sharply out of the ground. Nikola realized how dangerous it had been for him to be in the cave all alone.

The cavern took several more turns before they saw sunlight appearing off in the distance. Finally, they reached the entrance on the ledge behind the waterfall. Although it was dark and misty behind the waterfall, the sudden brightness of the sun coming through the water made them all blink until their eyes adjusted to the light.

Once Nikola could see normally again, he realized his clothes and shoes were tattered, wet, and dirty. "My mother is going to be so mad at me," he said to Ebby as he shivered in the cool air. He had not taken any food or water with him when he left and was hungry, thirsty, cold, and wet.

Ebby knew Nikola could not climb down the side of the cliff in his weakened condition. She asked him to give her Sofia's tear. It had lost nearly all its glow. Remembering what Sofia said to her before she and Skrufty started searching for Nikola, Ebby held the tear next to her heart and concentrated on Sofia. It started to vibrate and made a noise similar to the sound Sofia used to tear down the wall on Zidani Island. "It's working!" Ebby exclaimed.

"What's working?" asked Nikola.

In her rush to get Nikola safely out of the cave before the light died, Ebby did not tell him about Sofia. Before Ebby could answer him, Sofia burst through the waterfall and landed on the ledge next to her. Nikola let out a yelp and was about to run back into the cave. It was unbelievable to have been saved by Ebby, Skrufty, and a bunch of olms, but he certainly was not expecting a purple dragon to materialize out of nowhere too.

Before Nikola could bolt, Ebby shouted, "Wait! Sofia is my friend." Nikola froze in disbelief. "It's true, Nikola. I brought her to Slune to meet you. When we discovered you were missing, Sofia helped us find you by giving us the diamond that lit our way. She's been waiting down below with your parents. She'll take us to them."

Nikola was speechless as Ebby's words sank in. Ebby found Sofia, the magical purple sea dragon and brought her back to Slune to meet him. The same dragon he tried to catch with a string tied to a stick. And now, because he foolishly explored the cave by himself and got lost, he was the last person in the village to meet Sofia instead of the first. He wanted to cry again but Sofia had seen enough sadness for one day.

She introduced herself to Nikola and told him everything would be all right. Her voice was so gentle and lovely Nikola felt better right away. Ebby retrieved the ring she found in the first cavern and gave it to Nikola. "This is for you, Nikola. I know you wanted to bring back something special to show your friends."

The ring had three sapphires surrounded by diamonds set in a rich band of gold. Nikola thanked Ebby meekly and put it in his pocket. He no longer thought it was important to show off to his friends.

Sofia lifted Nikola, who was cradling Skrufty and Ebby in his arms, and approached the waterfall. "Hold on!" she said, diving straight down the waterfall. As she hurtled towards the ground, she flapped her wings as hard as she could. She broke free of the waterfall and swept straight up and out of danger. As soon as she was out into the air she flew towards the villagers gathered below. She landed next to Nikola's parents and set him down in front of them.

CHAPTER THIRTY

The Castle in the Clouds and the Dragon Tree

(In which Skrufty takes Sofia and Ebby to the castle in the clouds.)

Victoria and Alex rushed to Nikola hugging him so tightly he thought he was going to break. His mother was so relieved to see him she did not even scold him for getting lost or for destroying his clothes. They thanked Ebby, Sofia, and Skrufty for finding him while the villagers clapped and cheered.

Nikola's friend Deni asked, "Did you find anything, Nikola? Did you find the treasure?" The crowd grew quiet.

Nikola was about to reply when Victoria interrupted and told Deni she wanted to get Nikola cleaned up and fed before he told his story. The villagers were disappointed but knew she was right. Nikola was tired and dirtier than usual. He also smelled worse than he usually did after he played in the woods with his friends. Victoria suggested everyone meet in the main village square a few hours later and she would let Nikola tell them everything.

Alex invited the three rescuers to come with them to town. Ebby declined, knowing Sofia was too big to fit in their house and Nikola needed some rest. Plus, Ebby could not wait to tell Sofia everything that happened in the cave. She told Alex they would meet them in the square later. Once the villagers were out of sight, Ebby said, "I'm starving!!! Rescuing little boys from dark wet caves is hard work!"

Sofia smiled from ear to ear. "I'm starving too!"

Skrufty brought up the tail end of the conversation. "Let's go to the Dragon Tree at the castle in the clouds! There's plenty of grass and flowers for Ebby to eat, and I have a couple of tasty morsels *squirreled* away there too."

Sofia picked them up and flew towards the castle on the mountain where Skrufty knew of a Dragon Tree. The castle, Skrufty told them as they flew up to the top of the mountain, was called Drivenik Castle. It had been built a thousand years earlier by the same ancient people who built Slune. One of the first ancient men to live in the castle was named Dragoljub, which meant "dear love" in the ancient language.

"That must be why you are called 'dragons', because you are so special!" Ebby exclaimed. Skrufty had the same thought. Sofia was the loveliest, dearest creature he had ever met.

Skrufty told them more about the castle. "It hasn't been used for hundreds of years. The roof and floors were made of wood and rotted and collapsed long ago. Only the thick stone walls are still standing."

Sofia flew over the castle so they could view it from above. A round tower stood on each corner. Each tower faced out in a different direction. The castle did not have any windows. Long narrow slits were cut into the top of the towers and in some of the walls. "Why are there slits in the walls?" Ebby asked. "It doesn't look like anything could fit through them."

Skrufty was not sure. "I think it was so the people who lived there could throw flowers and nuts down to the bunnies and squirrels living nearby." Ebby was pleased the ancient people loved bunnies and squirrels.

Sofia landed near the castle. The ground around the castle was full of tasty flowers. Ebby's stomach growled. She was hungry, but she did not want to eat before Sofia located the Dragon Tree. "Where is the Dragon Tree, Skrufty?" Ebby asked.

Skrufty pointed to a spot just around the corner from the largest tower and said, "Follow me. I'll take you to it." With Skrufty jumping from spot to spot in the tall grass, Sofia and Ebby followed closely behind. Ebby did not think she had ever seen a Dragon Tree and did not know what to expect. The Dragon Tree was old—probably as old as the castle itself. The bark was gnarled and torn. Several of the branches were broken, leaving behind dark scars and jagged wood. A large hole sank deep into the ground close to the bottom of the trunk. Ebby recognized it as the same type of tree where Soto hid the hammer and bell he used to call Sofia. It dawned on Ebby that had been a Dragon Tree too.

Sofia went to the tree and reached down into the hole. She fished around until she pulled out a large pink and green fruit. It had sharp pointy thorn-like spikes sticking out of the rind.

It was oval and a little bigger than Sofia's eggshell. She smiled as she held it up. "This is Dragon Fruit. It's extremely rare. Unlike most other fruit, Dragon Fruit grows on the inside of the tree. It's delicious, but only dragons can eat it. I can tell that no other dragons have been to this tree for a long time because the hole is full of fruit. There's more food here than I can possibly eat.

"Skrufty, please get some nuts for yourself. Ebby can have flowers while I eat my Dragon Fruit. We'll sit in the shade of this tree, and you can tell me what happened in the cave." Skrufty dashed off to find his stash of nuts.

Ebby could not figure out how Sofia could eat Dragon Fruit without hurting her mouth. She realized she had never seen Sofia eat before. Sofia always flew off by herself when she ate.

Sofia sat under the tree and held the Dragon Fruit in her claws. She tore off the tough green and pink spikes with her teeth and spat them on the ground. Once she had removed all the spikes, she held the fruit up to show it to Ebby. The flesh underneath the spikes was bluish purple. It was juicy, and some of the juice dripped down Sofia's claws. Sofia took a big bite of the Dragon Fruit, and juice flowed down her chin as she chewed. She let out a big sigh and smiled. She was finally relaxed after everything that had happened in the past several days.

Ebby smiled back at Sofia and watched her eat. Just like Sofia, the Dragon Fruit looked scary at first but was soft, sweet, and tender inside. For the first time since Ebby met her, Sofia was absolutely at peace, like she did not have a care in the world. Helping find Nikola showed the people of Slune they had nothing to fear from Sofia. This was the one thing Sofia wanted more than anything, and Ebby helped her get it.

Ebby found some purple flowers growing under the Dragon Tree and nibbled on them. They tasted great, and soon her tummy stopped growling. Meanwhile, out of the corner of her eye Ebby detected Skrufty digging furiously not too far away. She overheard him saying to himself, "I am certain this is where I left that nut." He then scampered over to another spot and started digging there. He shook his head in frustration when he came up empty-handed again. He jumped to a third spot and dug there. Little scoops of dirt flew behind him as he scraped the ground. Still, he had no luck. He did this several more times before he finally found a big walnut buried a few inches under the soil.

Skrufty proudly carried the walnut over to the Dragon Tree and held it up for them to see. It was covered with mud and had been buried in the dirt for a long time. "I told you I have the best stash of nuts in the Land of Stones!" he said proudly.

Ebby and Sofia smiled and kept eating their meals. They were glad Skrufty found something to eat and thankful they did not have to eat it too. The ground was covered everywhere with little holes. Skrufty pointed at the field he just dug up. "See? That's why I keep most of my nuts in the cave behind the waterfall! I never lose them there!"

Sofia retrieved a second Dragon Fruit from the tree and started peeling it as Ebby shared their adventures in the four caverns. Skrufty dug into the nutshell for bits of walnut to eat as Ebby talked about the first cavern and the treasure inside. Sofia guessed it could have belonged to the Leavers after they left the Beginners on Zidani Island. They might have left it there for safekeeping and then forgot about it. They were called the Leavers, after all.

Next Ebby described Skrufty's cavern and his enormous collection of nuts. Ebby told Sofia if she was searching for something truly valuable to take home to her family, she would have stopped exploring the cave after finding Skrufty's nuts. "There is nothing else like it in the world!" Ebby exclaimed. Skrufty paused nibbling on his walnut long enough to beam with delight as Ebby said this.

Sofia was enchanted by Ebby's description of the third cavern and meeting Solomon and the olms. She had never met an olm before and had no idea the light from her tear could make an olm's skin turn blue and green. At first, she wondered what it would be like to never see the sun or moon or anything else outside the cave. Then she pictured the beautiful cave with the waterfall, the rainbow caused by the light from her tear, and the rocks hanging from the ceiling. She could fly to the tallest mountains and swim to the bottom of the deepest seas, but she would never be able to meet Solomon or see his home. Some places would have to live in her imagination.

Ebby described next how she and Skrufty used the chain of olms to go through the underwater opening into the fourth cavern. Sofia stopped eating her Dragon Fruit and became quiet when she recognized how risky it had been for them to swim so close to where the river dropped away into the darkness. "Ebby, you are brave. You are a true and loyal friend. The olms were kind to help you, but you must promise me never to do something like that again. I could not bear to lose you."

Ebby did not think she would need to use an underwater

chain of olms again. She promised Sofia she would always be careful, but she did not consider what she had done to be particularly dangerous.

After they ate as much as they wanted, Sofia licked the juice from the Dragon Fruit off her face and claws so she would be presentable for the people of Slune. She wanted to make a good impression on them. Seeing Sofia clean herself up, Skrufty wiped the bits of mud and dirt off his face. When they were spotless, Sofia flew them all back to the main square in Slune to meet Nikola and the other villagers.

CHAPTER THIRTY-ONE

Nikola's Journey in the Cave as Told by Nikola

(In which Nikola tells the people of Slune about getting lost in the cave.)

Nikola was all cleaned up when he and his parents arrived at the main square in Slune to tell the village about his misadventures. His face had been scrubbed, his hair was neatly combed, and his clothes were fresh and unwrinkled. Before he addressed the crowd that had gathered to hear his story, he ran to Ebby, picked her up, and rubbed noses with her. He put her down and told Skrufty that his mother had a surprise for him. Skrufty jumped around excitedly and twitched his tail in anticipation.

Nikola held Sofia's diamond tear in his hand. It was nearly as big as his palm. Although it was no longer glowing, it shined brilliantly in the sun in the way only a dragon's diamond tear can. He offered it to Sofia. "Thank you for letting Ebby use this to bring me out of the cave. It was perfect for such a scary place."

"Please keep it as a memento of your adventure," Sofia replied. "It started out as a symbol of sadness but ended up being a symbol of hope and happiness. I can't think of a better home for it than with you." Victoria and Alex could not believe

Sofia gave the diamond to Nikola. Dragon tears were extremely rare and valuable. To Sofia, however, it was just a tear, and she knew where to get more.

Deni could not wait any longer and blurted out, "Hey, Nikola! What happened in the cave? Did you find the treasure?"

Before he started telling his story, Nikola first apologized to everyone in the village. "I'm very sorry for all the trouble I caused. I never meant for any of this to happen and I didn't think anyone would find out about it. I got mad when I was told I couldn't explore the cave. It seemed unfair to me since my friends and I found it in the first place. I thought you were all being silly and overly protective when you said it was not safe to explore the cave without proper tools and supplies. But you were all right, and I'm truly sorry." Nikola's voice cracked. The villagers, hearing the sincerity in Nikola's voice, nodded their heads in acceptance of his apology.

"I went to my bedroom after the meeting and tried to sleep. I couldn't stop thinking about the treasure. I was certain it was there. The moon was full. It was almost as bright as day outside. I thought it would be easy to go to the cave, find the treasure, and be home without anyone knowing I'd gone. I snuck down to the kitchen after my parents went to sleep. I got a candle and three matches and put them in a small leather bag to keep them dry inside the cave. Then I wrote a note to my parents so they wouldn't worry if I didn't get home before they woke up.

"I ran to the waterfall without anyone seeing me and climbed up to the ledge where the cave is. I put the bag with the candle and matches under my shirt before I darted through the waterfall. I got a little wet, but everything inside the bag stayed dry. The moon barely lit up the mouth of the cave so I pulled out the candle. I broke the first match trying to light it. I wasn't concerned because I still had two matches left. I never needed more than two matches to light a candle, and I had brought three just in case.

"I lit the candle with the second match. The flame made the shadows bounce around the walls so it looked like the cave was moving. I kept thinking something might be hiding in the darkness, but I wanted to find the treasure. I didn't think I would ever get another chance to find it on my own.

"The candle didn't light up the cave much. I could barely see the entrance of an inner cavern on my right. I went inside and yelled out my name a couple of times. The echo was great!" Nikola grinned sheepishly. The villagers laughed. They all did that when they entered a cave. A few of the boys started imitating an echo by saying "Nikola, Nikola, Nikola..." with their voice getting softer with each repetition. Ebby, Sofia, and Skrufty exchanged glances and shrugged. Must be a human thing, they concluded.

After the crowd quieted down, Nikola resumed his story. "At first I couldn't believe anyone was afraid to go into a cave. It was fantastic! Rocks dangled from the ceiling and jutted up out of the floor, just like I had read about in school. I remembered the ones coming from the ceiling are called stalactites and the ones growing up from the floor are called stalagmites, but I'd never seen a real one before. They were all different shapes and sizes.

"The flame lit up everything close to me but beyond that it was completely dark. The air was cool and damp and smelled stuffy, like an old basement. I walked a few minutes and made several turns until I couldn't hear the waterfall any longer. I wasn't worried though. I thought I could turn around anytime I wanted and go back the same way I came in.

"The cave continued forever and there were all sorts of different paths and small rooms jutting off from the tunnel I was in. I came to a place where there were hundreds of small stalagmites growing together on the ground. They were thin and pointy. Water dripped constantly onto them from the ceiling and the ground was wet and slimy. I saw a sparkly flash close to the ground. I thought I found the treasure and moved closer. Before I could see what it was a drop of water landed on my candle and put out the flame." The villagers sighed and shook their heads.

"It was suddenly darker than anything you can imagine. It was the same if my eyes were opened or closed. I couldn't even see my hand right in front of my face. All I could hear was the sound of water dripping and echoing off the walls. It felt like the walls were coming closer.

"I knew the candle was wet so I made sure the wick was dry before I used the last match to light it. It took a couple of

minutes until it was dry enough. I looked for the shiny object once it was lit. I saw the sparkle again then realized it was just the candlelight playing off a wet spot on a rock. It wasn't the treasure. I explored a little bit more, but all I saw were rocks, shadows, and water.

"Being in the cave was no longer fun. I realized how big it was and how hard it would be for me to find anything in there by myself. There were a million places to hide a treasure. It was getting cold and I needed to get back home before my parents found out I was gone. I tried to figure out which way to go, but everything looked the same. I headed back the way I thought I came. Nothing was familiar. After a couple of bends and turns, I headed back the other way. When I thought I'd finally found the right way to get out of the cave, I spotted the burnt matchstick I'd thrown on the ground and realized I'd been going in circles. I was back at the spot where the candle went out." The crowd let out a collective groan.

"My candle was nearly gone and I didn't know what to do. I wished I'd listened to my parents." Nikola's voice cracked again as he expressed his regret. No one made a sound as Nikola paused in his story to hold back his tears. Alex placed his hand tenderly on Nikola's shoulder and encouraged him to keep going. Some of the parents hugged their children closer to them. A few of them wiped their eyes. Even though Ebby knew everything ended well, it still made her sad to know how frightened Nikola had been.

Nikola caught his breath for a moment as his lip trembled, and then he started again. "I passed the burnt matchstick and kept walking. I didn't know if I was going towards the entrance or deeper into the cave. After a few more minutes, the candle burnt itself out and I was left in total darkness. I tried to walk with my hands out in front of me but I kept bumping into things. The rocks were slimy and gross and it felt like all sorts of creepy crawly bugs were squirming around. I slipped on the ground a couple of times and was afraid I would fall down a hole or get hurt so I finally just sat down. I was cold and wet. I've never felt so alone in my life." He paused again and his mother gripped his hand reassuringly.

"Somehow I fell asleep. I don't know how long I slept. When I woke up it was still dark. I called out several times in case someone was trying to find me. All I could hear was the nonstop sound of water dripping. The echoes made me feel even more alone. I decided to stay where I was and wait for someone to find me like we do when we're playing Hide and Seek." Ebby smiled when Nikola mentioned playing Hide and Seek with her. She was grateful he had stayed in one place so she could find him.

"After a while I fell asleep again. It felt like I'd been in there for days and days. Finally, I heard someone call my name and saw a bouncing purple light in the distance coming towards me. As the light got closer I saw shiny blue and green creatures moving everywhere across the floor coming straight for me. I thought they were cave snakes and started to panic until I saw Ebby running towards me."

Overcome with emotion, Nikola paused again. Deni

shouted out impatiently, "Were they cave snakes?"

"No," Nikola replied, "they were special creatures called olms. They live in the cave and helped find me. I might still be in there if it wasn't for them. I thanked them, and then Ebby and Skrufty led me out of the cave with this." Nikola held up Sofia's tear for everyone to see. The crowd murmured in appreciation.

"Then, out of nowhere, Sofia burst through the waterfall. It nearly scared me to death! I thought for certain she was going to eat me! I was about to run back into the cave when Ebby stopped me and told me Sofia came to Slune to meet me. Can you believe that?" Nikola shook his head in astonishment. "Sofia picked us up and dove straight down into the waterfall and carried us to safety. That was the neatest thing that ever happened to me!" Sofia winked at him.

Nikola then addressed his rescuers. "Thank you for coming to find me. I'm sorry I messed up Sofia's return to Slune. I should have been here to meet you instead of being lost in the cave. I promise to listen to my parents next time."

Sofia responded, "I dreamed of returning to Slune for a long time. Although things didn't go exactly as I planned, I couldn't have asked for a better result. No one was hurt searching for you, you came home safely, and you learned from your mistake. Now that you have been found, we can all relax and get to know one another."

The villagers applauded Sofia's charming response. Everyone was grateful Nikola's adventure ended happily even if he had caused them a lot of worry. Now it was time for the people of Slune to turn their attention to celebrating Sofia's triumphant return.

Later that evening the villagers threw a big festival in honor of Sofia, Ebby, and Skrufty. They played music, danced, and ate until long after the sun went down. Nikola showed the villagers the ring Ebby gave him. Although the ring was beautiful, everyone agreed Sofia's tear was the real treasure. Nikola was so overwhelmed by being rescued and meeting Sofia he forgot to thank Ebby for the ring or ask where she found it. Since he only went inside the fourth cavern before getting lost, he did not find the treasure. Ebby decided not to tell Nikola about the treasure in the first cavern. She thought it would be more fun for him to find it on his own when he had proper equipment.

In the days that followed the villagers showed Sofia all the spectacular things she missed the first time she visited Slune. In addition, Skrufty took great pleasure in showing Sofia and Ebby around his forest and the surrounding areas. Skrufty received special treatment as well. Victoria made him delicious walnut bread and invited him to visit her when he wanted more. Skrufty, in turn, offered to bring Victoria walnuts from his secret stash whenever she ran out.

Ebby enjoyed every moment she spent in Slune. She knew Nikola would grow up to be a considerate person, surrounded by people who cared for him. Sofia was invigorated by the laughter she shared with her new friends. She no longer carried the burden or embarrassment of being rejected. After a few days Ebby and Sofia saw everything there was to see and did everything there was to do in Slune. They knew it was time to return to their journey. They still had other things they wanted to see and do together.

Even though Sofia normally did not eat bread, the villagers got together and made the biggest loaf of bread ever made in the Land of Stones to give to Ebby and Sofia on the morning of their departure. It took five men to carry it from the oven to the main square where they had built a special table for it. They smothered the bread with enough fresh butter and berries to feed the entire village. Sofia offered Ebby and Skrufty a piece of bread then ate the rest of the loaf in several bites, butter and jam dripping down her jaw. For Sofia, it was the perfect ending to the visit. She could not wait to go home and finally tell her grandfather everything she knew about Slune.

Ebby and Sofia said goodbye to everyone in Slune and headed for their next adventure.

CHAPTER THIRTY-TWO

Napoleon's Big Adventure

(In which Napoleon hears the wind sing in his ears again.)

Ebby often found herself thinking about Napoleon Ponyparte. Napoleon was warm and welcoming to Ebby at the beginning of her journey. He broadened her experiences by encouraging her to eat carrots and suggested she go to Slune to start her adventure. Going to Slune, in turn, led her to Nikola and then to all the friends and adventures that followed. His one act of kindness started everything. Now she wanted to return the thoughtfulness he had shown her. She was no longer in a rush to discover where the sun went at night. She knew it went everywhere. Most importantly she wanted Napoleon and Sofia to meet.

Napoleon lived on the other side of the mountains from Slune. It took Ebby almost two days to travel by bunny foot from his field to Slune. Sofia, however, could fly there in a few minutes.

Ebby and Sofia first spoke about visiting Napoleon when they were on Zidani Island. "Wouldn't it be fabulous for Napoleon to hear the wind sing in his ears again?" Ebby asked Sofia. Sofia knew exactly what to do, and now they were on their way to see him.

As Sofia flew over the mountains separating Slune from Fluffle Valley, Ebby watched the land pass below her. Nothing looked the same from the sky. When she left her fluffle, she thought it was the biggest place in the world. Now she knew it was tiny. The valley was covered with grass and flowers and she could not even tell where her fluffle was. She searched the fields until she spotted Napoleon. "There he is!" she said excitedly, pointing him out to Sofia.

Napoleon was busy eating tall blades of green grass and did not detect the purple dragon landing soundlessly behind him. Sofia learned long ago it was usually best for a dragon not to show up without a warning. She set Ebby down on the ground so she could approach Napoleon without Sofia scaring him. Ebby scooted as fast as she could and stopped next to Napoleon's fuzzy muzzle, which was close to the ground as he grazed on the grass. "Hi, Napoleon! It's me, Ebby. I'm back with my friend Sofia."

Napoleon blinked several times. He nickered quietly and softly shook his head. He did not hear Ebby approach him and thought he might be dreaming. He pulled his head back slightly to allow his eyes to focus on her standing in front of his nostrils. "Ebby, my dear sweet Ebby! You have grown so big! How have you been? Where did you come from?" He lowered his nose to the ground again, and Ebby rubbed her nose against it. It was just as soft as she remembered.

"I've been all over the Land of Stones, Napoleon! I made so many friends and saw such unbelievable places. I've thought about you many times, and I want you to meet my friend Sofia. She's standing behind you. Before you turn though, I want you to know you don't need to be afraid of her. She is the most kind and splendid dragon you will ever meet."

"Dragon?! Your friend is a dragon?" Napoleon snorted and spun around. He saw Sofia standing a short distance from him. Not only did a bunny sneak up on him, but a dragon landed in his field without his knowledge. He felt a little embarrassed for a second. This never would have happened when he was younger, he thought to himself. Napoleon completely forgot about feeling bad the moment he saw how excited Ebby was to see him. Her tail was moving a million times a second.

"What am I thinking?!" Napoleon said happily. "Of course you have a friend who's a dragon!" He whinnied a warm horse welcome towards Sofia. "You didn't tell me you were an Elusive Baby Bunny when we met, Ebby. I should have known, though. The kindness you showed me lifted my spirits like never before. I figured it out after you left. You were everything I ever heard about Elusive Baby Bunnies growing up, but I never imag-ined you were real. I thought you were make believe—just like dragons! And now I have an Elusive Baby Bunny and a dragon standing before me! Everyone will think I made this up, but I don't care! I hoped to see you again someday, Ebby, but I never thought I would. Elusive Baby Bunnies are elusive after all."

Sofia smiled as Napoleon spoke to Ebby. She had heard others say they did not know dragons and Elusive Baby Bunnies were real, as ridiculous as that sounded to her. "Hi, Napoleon." Sofia said. "I've heard wonderful things about you. Your kindness towards Ebby never left her heart. She carries it with her always." Sofia's voice was magical and soothing.

Ebby bounded over to Sofia and stood between her feet to show Napoleon he did not need to be afraid. Napoleon trotted behind. When they reached Sofia, Napoleon said, "You are magnificent, Ebby! Welcome to my home, Sofia. I am pleased to meet you."

The three of them settled comfortably in the grass. Napoleon asked Ebby to tell him about her adventures in the Land of Stones. She started by telling Napoleon about Nikola, including his recent rescue with the help of the olms. She told him about Frisky and her plans to become the first writer in all Foxdom. She continued telling him of all her and Sofia's adventures. Napoleon was enchanted by all the things Ebby had seen and experienced. Foxes, artists, flying with a dragon, underwater explorations, Zidani Island, olms, and cave rescues—it was all so unbelievable!

When Ebby was finished, Napoleon asked Sofia to tell him about her life. Sofia shared what it was like growing up as a dragon. It was quite a different world than the one Napoleon knew.

Napoleon reminded Sofia a lot of her grandfather, Seamus. Sofia understood why Ebby was so fond of him and why she wanted Sofia to meet him. Napoleon was patient and enjoyed learning new things. He also wanted to share what he had learned in his own life. She admired that about the older generations. They were always willing to share the lessons they had learned from their own experiences if you were willing to listen. What a spectacular source of treasure they held, just for the taking! Much more valuable than gold hidden in a cave, she thought.

Sofia asked Napoleon to tell her about his life. Napoleon told her how much he enjoyed being a horse. He loved running and playing with his friends when he was young. When he got older, he enjoyed working with Kristof. Napoleon was tall and strong and could pull a heavy cart with ease. When he was not working, Kristof rode him through the fields and visited nearby villages. Now he was slowing down a bit. Life was less hectic and consisted of the smaller pleasures in life like eating sweet juicy grass and feeling the warmth of the sun on his back. But mostly, he enjoyed the time spent visiting with friends.

Napoleon watched as Ebby and Sofia interacted with each other so naturally and marveled at Ebby's confidence. She was no bigger than a few small carrots bundled together but had the heart and courage of a dragon. Meeting Sofia had made Napoleon feel awkward for the first time in his life. Napoleon had always been bigger and stronger than anyone else, which made him confident in everything he did and everywhere he went. Now, standing next to a dragon several times bigger than he was, he understood how it felt to be smaller. He recognized how much effort Sofia made to set him at ease and make him feel comfortable rather than vulnerable. "Even an old horse like me can learn something new."

When they finished sharing their stories, Ebby asked Napoleon the one question she had waited forever to ask him. "Napoleon, how would you like to go flying with Sofia?"

Napoleon was speechless. In his entire life Napoleon never imagined he would be able to fly. The closest he had ever come to flying was when he jumped over a creek or fence and all four hooves left the ground at the same time. He loved the feeling of being weightless even if it lasted only for a moment. He had not felt that since he was young. Without hesitating he said, "I'd love to fly with you, Sofia. I'm certain it will be a little scary, but there is nothing I would rather do."

Sofia hoped Napoleon would say yes. She had wanted to take him flying ever since Ebby told her how much she thought Napoleon would enjoy it. "Let's go. Ebby can wait here and have something to eat. I don't want to worry about her when I'm focused on holding on to you."

Sofia explained how she intended to carry him so he would be comfortable and feel safe. She stood up on all four feet and asked Napoleon to position himself directly underneath her body. When he was standing under her, she started to flap her wings. Just as she lifted herself off the ground, she hugged Napoleon under his belly with her front legs and squeezed his haunches gently but firmly with her back legs. Although his front legs dangled freely below him, Napoleon felt like he was wrapped in a big blanket.

Sofia rose into the air above Napoleon's field. She asked him several times if he was comfortable. Each time Napoleon assured her he had never felt better in his life. Ebby watched from the ground as they went higher and higher. Sofia stopped climbing and circled around to fly over Fluffle Valley. When they were no longer in sight, Ebby began to eat the sweet green grass and yummy yellow flowers all around her. They tasted like home.

Napoleon, in the meantime, flew high above his field, past

the barn where he slept on rainy days, over Kristof's house, and beyond the valley where he spent most of his life. He felt the wind sing in his ears while blowing on his face, whiskers, and through his mane. He felt as light as a feather and as young as a colt. He saw the entire valley for the first time in his life. Sofia took him over neighboring fields and farms. Napoleon watched in amusement as the horses and cows spotted him flying overhead. They had no idea if what they were seeing was real or in their imagination.

Sofia then flew towards Slune. Napoleon watched breath-lessly as they climbed over the mountains and down into the valley on the other side. Sofia took him past the rivers and waterfalls that flowed through Slune. After flying over Drive-nik Castle, she asked Napoleon if he had ever been to the Big Sea. He had never gone that far, so Sofia followed the river all the way out. Once they were above the Big Sea, she flew over Roveen and showed Napoleon where Soto lived. Next, she flew over some of the Stone Islands so Napoleon could see how blue and clear the water was in the Big Sea.

She spotted a beautiful sandy beach on a remote uninhabited island and took Napoleon there. She let go of him just as his hooves touched the sand. Napoleon kicked up his heels and ran into the waves. He rolled around in the surf and got completely wet. When he stood back up, he ran down the shore chasing gulls who were trying to enjoy their lunch in "peace and quiet." Sofia watched Napoleon play on the beach and in the water with a sense of joy. There was absolutely nothing better in the world than bringing such happiness to a friend.

Napoleon had not felt this young and alive for a long time. After he ran up and down the beach several times, he trotted back to Sofia. "Sofia, you've given me an experience beyond my most fantastic dreams and have filled my heart with wonder. I will be able to reflect on this day for the rest of my life and know how it feels to have friends who love me."

Sofia wrapped a wing around Napoleon and nuzzled his nose with hers. As much as it meant to Napoleon, it meant just as much to Sofia to give him this memory. That was a lesson she had learned long ago: it was as fun to give a gift as it was to receive one.

Napoleon was covered with sand, seaweed, and salt water. Sofia did not want to take him back home like this. "Let's get you cleaned up." She picked him up again and headed back towards Slune. She flew to the big waterfall where Nikola got lost a few days earlier and landed in the pool at the bottom of the falls. Napoleon splashed around playfully for a few minutes until he washed all the sand and saltwater away. Sofia picked him back up, and they flew over the mountains again to his home. Napoleon was dry when they landed back in his field.

Ebby had fallen asleep after eating a bunch of yummy yellow flowers and was curled up in a ball under the warm sun. She was awakened by the swish of dragon wings and the sound of Napoleon's hooves landing on the ground. Napoleon sparkled and had a youthful glint in his eyes. He held his head high, and his mane flowed behind him. He strode towards her with a little more energy than she had seen from him before.

"How was it, Napoleon?"

"It was magnificent, Ebby, just like you knew it would be." Napoleon told Ebby everything about his adventure with Sofia. He was bursting with happiness. Ebby knew exactly how he felt. Sofia's boundless joy and kindness had the same effect on her.

That night Napoleon slept better than he had in a long time. He did not feel any aches or pains and dreamed about flying and playing in the ocean. The stars sparkled brightly in the sky overhead. They seemed to be celebrating.

CHAPTER THIRTY-THREE

Ebby's Return to Roveen

(In which Ebby and Sofia return to Roveen to visit Frisky and Soto.)

E bby and Sofia left Napoleon the next morning. Ebby had some unfinished business in Roveen, and Sofia offered to take her there. Ebby had promised Soto he could paint her and promised to tell Frisky about her adventures with Sofia.

They set out first to the island in the Big Sea where Sofia left her eggshell and Frisky's present. She picked the silk bag out of the Dragon Tree then proceeded to Roveen. It was lunch time when they landed at Soto's home. Soto sat in the shade under an olive tree eating some hard cheese, olives, and bread. His painter's smock was covered with brilliant specks of colorful paint. He smiled warmly as he heard Sofia arrive.

"Ah, there you are, my adventurous friends! I have been thinking about you."

Ebby dashed over to Soto, and he bent down to rub her ears. "My goodness, Ebby! You have grown so much!" Ebby did not feel any bigger than she did before, and she definitely did not feel any older. "There is something different about you. I can feel it. You are not the same Elusive Baby Bunny that came to Roveen. You have the dignity of a mighty dragon like Sofia."

"If I'm different," Ebby replied, "it's because Sofia showed me how easy it is to change the world with kindness and love even if I am small enough to fit in the palm of her hand."

Soto nodded his head thoughtfully as he rubbed his hand through his beard and smiled. "I hope your words are heard by everyone from one end of the world to the other."

Soto jumped up from his chair and exclaimed, "We need to let Frisky know you are here! She will be thrilled to see you and hear about your adventures. I know she will want to write about them. Ivan LeKar has been an excellent teacher. She is already writing her first book!"

Ebby suggested Soto finish his lunch. She would run to town, fetch Frisky from her writing studio at Ivan LeKar's house, and bring her back to Soto's farm. Sofia offered to fly her there, but Ebby suggested Sofia stay with Soto and keep him company. They had been flying all morning, and Ebby was ready to run around a bit.

Ebby found Frisky sitting outside in Ivan LeKar's yard staring at a blank piece of paper and lost in thought. Ebby snuck up on her from behind and pounced on her playfully. She knocked

Frisky over, just like Frisky did to her the first time they met. They rolled paw over tail and ended up sprawled on their backs in the grass a few feet away. Frisky sprang to her feet and flipped around to see who had jumped on her. When she recognized Ebby, she let out yips of joy and hugged her.

"I am so glad you came back, Ebby! I missed you. You're getting so big. I must be losing my fox instincts because I didn't hear you coming."

"You're getting bigger too! I want to hear about everything you've been doing since we left. What are you doing outside staring at a blank piece of paper? Can you come with me? Sofia and Soto are waiting for us. I have so much to tell you."

"I'm trying to write a book about my brother, Rip. I'm going to call it *Fox in the Rox*. It's about his adventures in the ruins where we live, but I'm stuck. I can't think about anything to write. Mr. LeKar always tells me to go outside and get some fresh air if I can't write. That's why I am out here staring at this piece of paper. But I'd much rather go with you to see Sofia!"

Frisky picked up the piece of paper she was staring at and put it on a small table. She set her pen down on top of the paper. Ivan LeKar taught her to always treat her belongings with respect. "Can I introduce you to Mr. LeKar before we leave? I told him about you, and he wants to meet you."

Ebby nodded her head and wiggled her tail rapidly. "Absolutely!"

Frisky led Ebby inside Ivan LeKar's home. It was a small two-story house with large windows that faced the Big Sea. The walls were covered with shelves containing books of every size. Many of them had Ivan LeKar's name written across the spine. "These are some of the books he's written." Frisky read some of the titles to Ebby: "*The Cabbage Gardener, A Small Town in the Land of Stones, The Sheepdog who Came in From the Cold,* and *Smelly People.*" Curious titles, Ebby thought to herself. *Smelly People* was probably about little boys considering how the olms were able to smell Nikola from a long distance away. She giggled quietly to herself.

Frisky led her down the hallway past a set of old worn leather-bound books. "You might find these interesting too. The title of these seven volumes is *Tails of an Elusive Baby Bunny.*" Ebby's heart skipped a beat. She wanted to examine them closer but Frisky called out "Come on, hurry up!" from down the hall.

Frisky took Ebby upstairs and into a room at the side of the house facing the sea. "Excuse me, Mr. LeKar," Frisky said, "my friend Ebby has come back from her travels, and I know you wanted to meet her."

A tall, slender, elderly man with white hair sat in a chair in front of a large desk covered with pieces of paper and books. He was in the middle of writing something. He smiled broadly, set his pen down, and put his hands on his knees so he could give them his full attention. His blue eyes sparkled in the sunlight shining through the window. His cheeks were bright pink, and his eyebrows reminded Ebby of Skrufty's tail—they were big and bushy with a life of their own. Ebby sensed he was smart and kind.

"It's an honor to finally meet you, Ebby. Frisky speaks highly of you. The kindness, friendship, and courage of Elusive Baby Bunnies are legendary. I have the complete set of

Tails of an Elusive Baby Bunny somewhere in this house. I nearly wore out the pages reading and re-reading them when I was a child. To be honest the stories sounded too good to be true, and I thought they were fairy tales until I was an adult.

"What made you change your mind?" Ebby asked.

"Over fifty years ago, rumors came to the Land of Stones about an Elusive Baby Bunny they called 'Rebby the Gallant' who was traveling through the Land of Dragons. I immediately dropped everything I was doing and tried to find him but, true to his name, he was too elusive. By the time the story about his amazing exploits became known in one place, he was already somewhere else. I was always one or two steps behind him. He left behind a path of dazzling events everywhere he went. Everyone he met was profoundly impacted by his kindness in one way or the other."

Chip and Spot had told Ebby the story about Rebby the Gallant saving a village from flooding by digging a tunnel under a large boulder. She was surprised that Ivan LeKar actually tried to find Rebby the Gallant. She asked Ivan whether he had heard that story before.

"Yes, that was one of my favorite stories," he replied. "I personally saw Rebby's Rock, and the boulder was even bigger than I pictured it. To this day I don't know how he managed to dig a tunnel under the boulder. He saved the entire village and no one was injured thanks to his quick thinking. There were many other stories about his bravery. Unfortunately, I never found Rebby. I always planned to write a book about him, but I got too busy writing other books when I came back from the Land of Dragons.

"I never heard about Elusive Baby Bunnies again until

Frisky told me about you. She mentioned wanting to write about your adventures during one of our lessons. I was so excited to meet you but she told me you had already left with a magical purple sea dragon. All the stories I read as a child came flooding back to me. I can't wait to hear about your adventures. I am certain they will be equally noteworthy."

Ebby did not think she had done anything unusual. When a friend was lonely or frightened, she comforted them. When they were lost, she helped find them. She was just being herself. "Isn't everyone like me?" Ebby asked Ivan.

"No, Ebby. Although everyone *could* be like you if they wanted, most don't know how. I don't know anything you have done since you left Roveen, but it's not often that a fox and a bunny become friends like you did."

"Everyone can be friends if they want to be," Ebby said. Ebby never met anyone she did not want as a friend. From Spot to Sofia, everyone she met had made her life better. She stood on her back legs and held her front foot out to Ivan, as was the custom among humans when first meeting someone new. He took it in his hand and affectionately shook it.

"That's the first step, isn't it?" Ivan said. "Just hold out your hand and see who takes it." Ebby wiggled her tail in agreement. "How did you hear about Rebby the Gallant?" Ivan asked. "I don't believe his story was ever written down."

Ebby told him she learned the story about Rebby the Gallant from a bug and chipmunk in Fluffle Valley. She did not know how Spot and Chip learned about Rebby, but she encountered many others in the Land of Stones who had heard of Elusive Baby Bunnies from their parents and grandparents. Ebby was intrigued by what Ivan said about trying to find Rebby the Gallant so he could write a book about him. She did not know anything about the history of Elusive Baby Bunnies other than what Chip and Spot had told her. She wanted to hear more about Rebby's adventures in the Land of Dragons.

Ebby thanked Ivan for taking Frisky into his home and teaching her how to read and write. Ivan smiled broadly and said, "Sharing my knowledge and skill with Frisky is one of the best things I have ever done. I love watching her learn. She is becoming a better writer every day."

Frisky appreciated that Ivan spoke so kindly about her progress, but she was frustrated. "I haven't been able write for several days," she said. "I stare at that blank sheet of paper for hours, but nothing comes to me. Maybe I wasn't meant to be an author, just like I couldn't feel being a painter in my heart."

Ivan bent over from his seat and spoke to Frisky in the kindest possible way. "It's usually not easy to become good at something, Frisky. Even after all these years, I still spend lots of time staring at blank pages hoping for the words to magically reveal themselves. You have a great deal of talent, and I can tell you want to tell stories. Maybe you just don't want to write a book about your brother. Now that Ebby is back, perhaps you can write the eighth volume of *Tails of an Elusive Baby Bunny* about her instead. A few days ago, I found my old box of notes about Rebby the Gallant in the attic. I haven't shown them to you yet. You can write about him too if you want."

Frisky perked up her ears and wagged her tail. She felt like a heavy weight had been lifted off her. Writing about Elusive Baby Bunnies sounded much more appealing than writing about her brother. "Now I have two books to write!" she exclaimed joyfully.

After speaking with Ivan a little longer, Ebby and Frisky ran all the way back to Soto's house. Soto and Sofia were still in the same place where Ebby left them. Frisky ran up to Sofia and licked her on the nose. "Welcome back, Sofia! Thank you for taking such good care of Ebby. She isn't afraid to try anything. I knew she would be fine, but I still worried about her occasionally."

Sofia did too. She had not forgotten Ebby's rescue of Nikola using the underwater "chain of olms" next to a roaring river that dropped off into the unknown.

"We have something for you, Frisky," Sofia said cheerfully. "We found it, and it reminded us of you." Frisky yipped excitedly and chased her tail in anticipation. Sofia pulled the golden scepter with the fox head out of the silk bag and held it out for Frisky to see. It was solid gold and Sofia knew Frisky would not be able to lift it by herself. The eyes in the scepter were made of deep blue sapphires and sparkled in the sun.

Frisky stopped running around and inspected the scepter. "It looks just like my mom! Thank you for thinking of me! It will remind me of our times together."

Sofia handed it to Soto. He was impressed. He could tell that it was old and valuable. "Where did you find it?"

They took turns telling Soto and Frisky about their underwater adventure. Ebby described the surprising variety of fishes and other sea creatures they saw. Sofia told them about the shipwreck, the golden treasure scattered across the sea floor, and the marble columns and statues.

Soto guessed the same ancient people who built Roveen probably lost the treasure.

This led Ebby to tell them about Zidani Island and the Tallers' and Leavers' possible connection to the treasure. Frisky and Soto listened to every detail of their story with delight. They loved hearing about Alotta Burrotta, Darko and Manuela, and how Sofia used the love in her heart to remove the wall and free the Tallers.

Sofia then bragged about how brave Ebby was to go into the four caverns to find Nikola and her experience with Solomon and the "chain of olms".

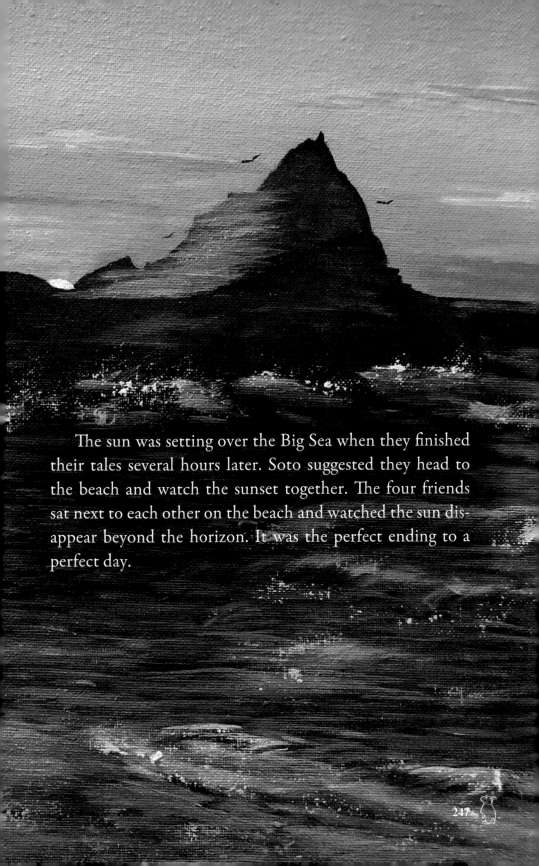

The sun was setting over the Big Sea when they finished their tales several hours later. Soto suggested they head to the beach and watch the sunset together. The four friends sat next to each other on the beach and watched the sun disappear beyond the horizon. It was the perfect ending to a perfect day.

CHAPTER THIRTY-FOUR

Ebby's Portrait

(In which Soto paints Ebby in a most magnificent way.)

The next morning Ebby and Frisky found Soto finishing his last bite of stale bread dipped in coffee. He had spent the night thinking about the best way to portray Ebby. After hearing about her adventures with Sofia the day before, he wanted her portrait to be as unique as she was, for she was no ordinary bunny.

Sofia joined them a short time later. She was licking the last bit of Dragon Fruit juice off her chin as she approached. They walked to Soto's studio in the back of his yard. Soto had already set up his easel, a canvas, paints, his palette, and a small stool in the yard. Frisky's golden scepter leaned against Soto's easel. Soto asked Ebby to get up on the stool and stand as upright as she could. "Ebby, I will paint a special portrait of you. Instead of painting you in a field of grass and flowers like Frisky, I want to paint you as others will remember you: as a magnificent leader."

Ebby did not know what he meant, but she knew he would paint from his heart, and that was all that mattered.

Soto started by painting the background first. He painted a background rich in gold and purple. Once he was finished with the background, he painted Ebby's eyes. The eyes, he noted, were the most important part of the face. He wanted to make Ebby's eyes warm and kind. They sparkled with brown and gold specks of paint. Finally, he captured the sky's reflection in her eyes with a careful dab of blue paint. Once he was certain the eyes exactly captured Ebby's personality, he started on the rest of her face.

Soto painted for several hours. Frisky asked Sofia and Ebby detailed questions about their adventures as he painted. She jotted down notes as quickly as she could. On occasion, as they answered Frisky's questions, Soto let out an exclamation of surprise or a little giggle. Ebby could not tell if he was commenting about her story or the portrait he was painting.

Finally, towards the end of the day, Soto announced he

was finished. Frisky and Sofia looked over his shoulder to see what he had done. "It's magnificent!" they said together. Ebby asked if she could see it too.

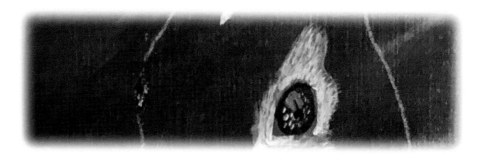

"Of course, my friend," Soto said. Ebby hopped off the stool where she had been posing for Soto's painting. Soto had painted Ebby in the style of the ancient people of the Land of Stones. She wore a red dress elaborately decorated with gold and jewels. A rich cape the color of the greenest grass rested on her shoulders. She held Frisky's golden scepter in one hand and a book titled *Fox in the Rox* in the other. Soto explained the scepter symbolized her adventures with Sofia and the book showed the impact Ebby had on Frisky's life. Frisky became a writer because Ebby invited her to travel with her to Roveen, something very few bunnies would have done to a fox who tried to eat her, Soto noted.

"I will call this painting *Ebby the Magnificent*," Soto proclaimed, "for you are truly magnificent, Ebby! The world will learn about your kindness, friendship, loyalty, and courage through Frisky's stories. And, if Frisky will allow me, I will paint your adventures to accompany her book."

Ebby was humbled by Soto's explanation of his painting and his offer to illustrate her adventures. "I couldn't have done any of this without friends like you," she said facing them.

"Your friendship is the only treasure I will ever need."

CHAPTER THIRTY-FIVE

The Way Home

(In which Ebby goes back to her fluffle.)

The four friends spent several more days together enjoying each other's company and making plans to get together again in the future. Frisky started writing Ebby's story instead of finishing the book about Rip. No amount of fresh air was helping her write more about her brother, but she had pages of notes about Ebby. She loved Rip, but Ebby's story needed to be told. She proudly read the first sentence of her book: "In a beautiful valley full of flowers and tall, sweet grass lived a baby bunny named Ebby." Ebby, Sofia, and Soto unanimously agreed it was a brilliant beginning. "It took me all night to write that one sentence!" Frisky said, shaking her head and laughing.

Soto used some of his time to finish a few of Sofia's paintings. He made a special point to tell Sofia she had also changed greatly since they first met many years earlier. Sofia had never been happier, and it showed. Her eyes sparkled even brighter than they had before. It was clear to Soto that her friendship with Ebby and her successful visit to Slune had liberated her and lifted her spirits.

Ebby decided it was time to return to Fluffle Valley. She

had been gone a long time and missed her family and friends. As much fun as it had been to explore the Land of Stones, a part of her longed to be back in her familiar home, at least until she got the urge to go somewhere else.

Sofia was also eager to return home and finally tell her grandfather about Slune. She offered to fly Ebby home on her way back to the Land of Dragons. Ebby was elated because she wanted everyone in the fluffle to meet Sofia. She hoped they would come out of their hiding places to meet her.

As Ebby and Sofia got ready to leave, Soto gave Ebby a small paper bag filled with something inside. He said it was a gift for Ebby's mother. Ebby opened the bag and saw the most beautiful carrots she had ever seen. "I picked them this morning from my garden. You mentioned you wanted to take some carrots home to your mother when you were talking with Frisky. I hope she enjoys them."

Ebby thought about her mother each time she ate a carrot. This was the perfect present to give her.

Frisky ran up to Ebby, and they rubbed noses and hugged each other. "I'll let you know when I finish the book. I am going to call it *Ebby the Magnificent: Tails of an Elusive Baby Bunny.*" Ebby was a little embarrassed to be called "magnificent", but she thought the title was excellent. "Maybe when I finish your book I will start the book about Rebby the Gallant," Frisky said.

Sofia lowered her right hand to the ground so Ebby could climb into her palm while holding the bag of carrots. Sofia held the silk bag containing her eggshell in her left claw. She flapped her wings and they rose steadily into the sky. Ebby waved at Soto and Frisky until she could no longer see them.

As Sofia flew over the Big Sea, Ebby gazed at the sparkling blue water below her. She thought about the times she had stared out across the water on her trip to Roveen hoping for a glimpse of the magical purple sea dragon she first heard about in Slune. Now she was flying with her! She thought about some of the friends she made along the way: Frisky, Napoleon, Bud Der, and Racket. She smiled thinking about George C. Gull and the funny trick she and Sofia had pulled on him.

The closer she got to her home, the more excited and sadder she got. She looked forward to seeing her mother and friends but was sad about saying goodbye to Sofia and their adventures coming to an end. She told Sofia how she was feeling. It was hard to express how she could be so happy and sad at the same time.

"That's the trouble with finishing anything you have enjoyed," Sofia said. "It's always that way when something you like comes to an end. The best way to stay happy is to remember all the special things that happened and think about all the breathtaking things that will happen in the future. Although it may seem like we are coming to the end of our adventure, always remember there is friendship, sunshine, and happiness waiting for us just beyond the next turn."

THE END...OR IS IT THE BEGINNING?